W9-ADZ-466

J. A. Whitford
& the Great California
Gold Hunt

J. A. Whitford
& the Great
California Gold Hunt

FRANK RODERUS

A DOUBLE D WESTERN
DOUBLEDAY
New York   London   Toronto   Sydney   Auckland

A Double D Western
PUBLISHED BY DOUBLEDAY
a division of Bantam Doubleday Dell Publishing Group, Inc.
666 Fifth Avenue, New York, New York 10103

Double D Western, Doubleday,
and the portrayal of the letters DD
are trademarks of Doubleday, a division of
Bantam Doubleday Dell Publishing Group, Inc.

Library of Congress Cataloging-in-Publication Data

Roderus, Frank.
J. A. Whitford & the great California gold hunt / Frank Roderus.
—1st ed.
p.   cm.—(A Double D western)
1. California—Gold discoveries—Fiction. I. Title. II. Title:
J. A. Whitford and the great California gold hunt.
PS3568.O346J14 1990
813'.54—dc20   90-32473
CIP

ISBN 0-385-26690-1

I

The Setup

ONE

AH, THIS WAS WONDERFUL. This was life. This was commerce. This was *opportunity*.

Surrounded by such marvelous activity. Such wonderful sights.

Ships' rigging stark against the pale sky. Shouts and laughs and curses. Longshoremen straining to shift the burdens of entire nations. Sweating workmen side by side with handsomely attired gentlemen. Kegs and bales and bundles moving inside the massive cargo nets. Crane booms swinging and cabled tackle groaning.

The sharp, keen scents of . . . well, never mind that. The East River wharf stank of coal smoke and sewage. The invigorating salt air would presumably come later.

This was life as it was meant to be lived. This was . . . too dang early in the morning, actually.

J. Aubrey belched—the second-hand taste somewhat less pleasant than last night's initial experience had been—and made a face.

This was practically the crack of dawn, was what it was. Ten o'clock, anyway. Entirely too early to contemplate.

On the other hand, a gentleman *did* want to make a living. And today . . .

He rubbed his hands together in anticipation of what this day would bring, and stepped boldly into the kiosk that he'd rented for the past two weeks, two dollars per week, outrageous. An investment, however. An investment against the future.

The tidily lettered sign was already in place.

"WHITFORD EXPEDITION" in large print; "To The Newest Baja Discoveries" slightly smaller; "Sailing The 14th Inst. In This Year 18 and 52 Aboard *Yucatán Princess*, Capt.

A. V. Baker Commanding," this latter portion written quite small indeed.

The sign had cost nothing but a bit of paint and a few moments of time. It was truly remarkable the way free enterprise could operate in a civilized society. Wonderful.

J. Aubrey Whitford spread his ledger open on the narrow board that served as a counter, and rubbed his hands together again in eagerness.

Ah, what marvels this day would bring.

He tugged at his coattails and fingered his collar and flicked at his lapels. A gentleman should present himself at his best on a day so fine as this.

J. Aubrey wore a maroon cutaway with modest, square-cut tails. Yellow brocade vest. Dove-gray breeches. Calfskin pumps. Kidskin gloves. Gleaming silk top hat. Except for the hat—J. Aubrey was particular about his hats, regardless of other circumstances—the clothing had seen better days. No matter. A deposit had already been laid with the tailor.

Besides, it was the man quite as much as the clothing that mattered. Or nearly so, depending. And J. Aubrey had no doubts about that aspect of his appearance.

He was taller than average, even if a sometimes depressing half inch short of an even six feet. He had been graced with naturally broad shoulders, a narrowness of hip, flatness of stomach and thickness of limb. His physique was not deemed unattractive by members of the fairer sex.

More important, J. Aubrey Whitford had a face and a demeanor that incited the full faith and confidence of man and woman alike.

His head was leonine, which is to say slightly overlarge for his body. His hair was thick and full and brown, sweeping down into muttonchop side whiskers, his face otherwise freshly shaven. He would be glad when some gray would finally begin to appear at his temples. Gray temples are quite distinguished.

His eyes were wide-set and brown, and lightly flecked with a peculiar shade of brilliant gold. Clear and open and silently speaking of honesty and integrity. The sort of eye a man can look into and give back trust. The sort of eye a lady can look into and lose herself within. His eyes, J. Aubrey always thought, were among his best features.

His nose was long and straight and regular. His jaw line was square and solid, much too firm to be covered with a mat of beard. Beards are distinguished, true, but they can be used to hide so much else. It would have been a true and rueful waste to cover over the cleft at chin-point that gave J. Aubrey such a craggy, manly look.

His eyebrows were bushy and full, the texture of his skin unmarred by pox or pitting.

J. Aubrey Whitford looked every inch the gentleman of perception and leisure. An orator, perhaps. A philosopher. A leader of men.

J. Aubrey preferred to think of himself, however, as a humble entrepreneur.

He rubbed his hands together yet a third time and reached from long habit for the vest pocket where a bulbous watch normally resided. The habit failed him this time, however. He had his chain and fob but no watch. He had quite forgotten the recent necessity to pawn the item.

He grunted and settled for smoothing down the front of the vest.

The missing watch was of no importance. This very evening he would retrieve it. Better, he would replace it. The old article was brass cased with an overlay of gilt, washed but not filled. This very evening he could replace it with a more suitable watch. Something in a genuine gold case came to mind, perhaps with artistic engraving. A hunt case, then. And an inscription within? Perhaps. Although that made things more difficult to pawn afterward. No inscription, then. J. Aubrey Whitford was as much the realist as he was the eternal optimist. No personalized inscription, most definitely.

He cleared his throat and made a face, drawing his lips back from white, even teeth to rub a forefinger quickly over his teeth and gums. It wouldn't do to allow a bit of cabbage, say, to interfere with an otherwise outstanding appearance.

Not that he'd had cabbage recently. Or so much of anything else if the truth be known. A meager bowl of porridge for his supper last night. Followed by a libation or two. One did have to establish priorities, after all. Breakfast had been a cup of water and the knowledge that tonight his circumstances would be improved.

He shot his jaw, tugged at his cuffs and waited in growing anticipation for the first of his, um, expeditionary clients to arrive for boarding.

TWO

"AH YES. Mr. Bolliger. So happy to see you today, sir. Let me see here." J. Aubrey ran a pencil tip ostentatiously down the list written in the ledger before him, made a small tick mark beside Bolliger's name and beamed across the counter at the gentleman in question. "The balance due, sir, is four hundred twenty-eight dollars, I believe."

Bolliger dutifully counted out the money and laid it on the counter.

It was all J. Aubrey could do to keep from bursting into joyous song or yelps of excitement.

He kept his expression devoid of joy, however, and permitted only a casual and placid geniality to show.

"Very good, sir. No, don't turn away yet, please. You will need your ticket for boarding the *Yucatán Princess.* And of course your receipt. Can't allow you to get away without a receipt, can I? We must observe the proprieties, by all means."

J. Aubrey smiled and nodded, and tried to contain the glee that bubbled within his chest as he bent to retrieve the briefcase that served as his office.

"Just one moment, sir. One moment only."

He dug through the cluttered contents of the leather case and pulled out a pad of preprinted receipt forms. He filled one out, signed it, and with a flourish presented to Mr. Haywood Bolliger one properly endorsed receipt and one pasteboard ticket admitting him passage on the *Yucatán Princess,* Captain A. V. Baker commanding.

Those pasteboards had cost him a depressing amount of front money in printing costs.

But there again it was sheer investment. And a nice touch to boot.

Lent confidence in the business enterprise, after all.

And assured one and all—J. Aubrey Whitford in particular—
that each of his paying expedition members would be aboard
the great ship *Yucatán Princess* when she spread her sails.

That, J. Aubrey conceded happily to himself as he shuffled
Bolliger's coins into neat piles and slid them from countertop to
briefcase interior, was a stroke of purest genius.

If he did say so himself.

Anyone else, any shortsighted cad who tried to play the game,
why *anyone* else at all would have done the obvious.

Greed, J. Aubrey always said. Greed is the downfall of hu-
mankind.

Never let it be said that J. Aubrey Whitford is, was or would
be a greedy man.

No, sir.

A greedy man would have taken all the traffic would bear and
then tried to pocket all of it for himself.

But not J. Aubrey Whitford. No, sir.

A greedy man would have left his clients anxious and angry
on the East River wharf.

Never J. Aubrey.

J. Aubrey had gone to the actual trouble and expense of hir-
ing a genuine ship and her captain.

She lay to a mooring out there at this very moment.

Her lighter stood by even as J. Aubrey and Bolliger spoke,
ready and willing to take the gentleman aboard, and all his luggage with him.

Hence the pasteboards. Hence, in fact, the twenty-eight dollar balance owing on the passage fees for Mr. Haywood Bolliger.

The fee, every penny of it, would be paid into the hand of
Capt. A. V. Baker.

Every paid-up passenger would be duly loaded aboard the
fine ship *Yucatán Princess.*

Baker would be happy. The expedition members would be

happy. The ship would sail on the tide and see land no more for days and days and days to come.

Then J. Aubrey could happily, and safely, pocket his proceeds and go about his affairs.

By the time any of his expedition members became the wiser, why, they would be far off to sea and quite unable to return.

Sheer genius was what it was. J. Aubrey congratulated himself once more.

Probably no man since the commencement of time had ever given himself such a head start as this one.

Genius.

J. Aubrey shook Bolliger's hand and pointed out the waiting lighter not a hundred feet away, and smiled a greeting to the next of the expedition's eager members.

"Mr. Hankins, is it not, sir? So happy to see you today, Mr. Hankins. Let me find you on my list here. Yes, right here you are, sir." He made the tick mark, consulted the appropriate ledger column and smiled once more. "You have a balance owing, Mr. Hankins, of four hundred twenty-three dollars."

It was all J. Aubrey could do to keep his excitement contained.

Twenty-seven expedition members with deposits already laid and tickets ready. Four hundred dollars clear and certain profit from each and every one of them. In excess of ten thousand dollars in toto. Ten thousand and eight hundred, to be precise.

J. Aubrey wondered if this venture might establish a record, a historic benchmark against which all other scams must pale.

A personal record certainly. No question about that. But an all-time record? He would have to look into it. At his leisure. Of which he would have plenty just as soon as the *Yucatán Princess* was safely to sea.

A small laugh escaped him as he counted Mr. Junius Hankins' cash payment in full into the depths of the briefcase, and handed over the receipt and ship boarding ticket in return.

Oh, it felt wonderful to be alive this day.

THREE

J. AUBREY could not *believe* his good fortune. A sign, obviously. A portent. A reward for clean living? He laughed aloud and patted the bulging, incredibly heavy briefcase.

Smith—the name on the passenger list was a pathetically transparent alias, but no matter—had actually brought two friends with him. Paying friends with cash in hand. Two. Eight hundred dollars in handsome and unexpected profit for this finest of all days.

There hadn't even been tickets for them, but that was all right. J. Aubrey had sent a note out to the ship by way of the lighter. Baker was expecting payment and would provide passage for the unexpected but quite welcome two. Wonderful.

J. Aubrey rubbed his hands together—out of sight of the expedition members assembled on the wharf nearby, of course—and watched as the small lighter returned for another load.

It was amazing the amount of equipment some of the gentlemen were carrying with them for their Baja adventure.

Picks, shovels, gold pans, patent rocker and riffle mechanisms. Foodstuffs? In abundance. Flour, cornmeal, salt pork, salt beef, bacon and ham. Salt, sugar, raisins and dried fruits. Coffee and tea. They must have spent a fortune outfitting themselves. J. Aubrey wished now that he'd thought to offer provisions for the expedition. At a price, of course. It was something to keep in mind for the future.

He smiled in spite of that late discovery.

Eleven thousand six hundred. In cash. In hand. In the briefcase that rested so snug and heavy against his ankle.

Incredible.

Baker's passage fees he held in a separate pouch atop the counter that he would so soon vacate for the last time.

The lighter reached the wharf, and a barefooted sailor leaped nimbly onto the planks to tie the small craft securely fore and aft. Then Capt. Baker himself was helped onto terra firma.

J. Aubrey had been expecting him. Looking forward to the captain's arrival, in fact. J. Aubrey could not safely abscond until the passage fees were paid and the ship under sail.

He smiled and rubbed his hands together as Baker approached the kiosk.

Wonderful.

A few of the passengers waiting to board trailed along with him, drat it, while their luggage was being loaded into the lighter.

"Captain. Good to see you, sir."

Baker grunted. He was a taciturn sort, and unfriendly. But amenable to the lure of cash, the greedy rascal. J. Aubrey had had to bargain with him for hours to arrange this deal, juggling Baker's demands against the safety of distance. They had determined in the end on passage paid through to some port in the distant south. Augustine, Baker called it, except that sometimes he referred to it as Marion. J. Aubrey neither knew nor cared where it was. It was sufficiently far and the *Yucatán Princess* would not make landfall again until she reached it; that was the extent of J. Aubrey's concern.

"You got my money, Whitford?"

With a smile and a genteel bow, J. Aubrey pushed the weighty pouch across the counter to the captain. "In full, sir."

"I'll count it here."

"Of course." J. Aubrey looked past Baker's shoulder and gave a wink to the several expeditioners who stood there.

The ship's captain opened the pouch, poured out a glittering cascade of gold coin and laboriously began to count them into piles.

One of the marks, a man named Field, pressed closer. "The captain says you aren't boarding with us, Mr. Whitford?" He sounded angry. Or prepared to be. Mildly suspicious at this point.

J. Aubrey's smile never wavered. Smoothly, easily, he explained. "I have to exchange our cash for bank drafts, Mr. Field. It wouldn't do to risk spoiling our venture if we were to fall afoul of brigands. No, sir, I shall secure our drafts and take the pilot boat to meet you aboard, never fear. We are all in this together, ha ha. Thick and thin. Share and share alike, Mr. Field. From now until we all return as rich as Croseus."

Foresight was ever important. J. Aubrey gave close attention to detail, and this was his reward. He tried at all times to prepare himself against any question.

Field grunted. He seemed satisfied enough.

And the captain, standing right there and hearing the whole thing, offered neither objection nor correction. J. Aubrey had had sense enough to negotiate an unpaid passage for himself providing at least twenty expedition members bought passage.

Foresight.

It was ever invaluable.

J. Aubrey smiled with a serene and unfeigned confidence while the captain counted out the passage money, offered accurate to the very penny, and declared himself satisfied with the arrangement.

"Soon as the last of that junk is aboard we can weigh anchor," Baker conceded.

"I shall be along on the boat that fetches your pilot, sir," J. Aubrey said easily.

Baker shrugged and turned away to scowl at his sailors.

The expeditioners trudged meekly along behind.

And J. Aubrey Whitford happily nudged the briefcase on the ground beside him.

The weight of all that gold coin made the case actually too heavy to comfortably shift aside.

What a delightful problem for a gentleman to have.

J. Aubrey watched with an air of benign good will, as the last of the luggage was handed into the lighter and the last of his expedition members descended into the boat.

The lines were cast off, and the sailors scrambled agilely

aboard. J. Aubrey lost sight of them beneath the level of the wharf for a few moments, then picked them up to view again as the sailors strained against the oars and the lighter pulled for the ship lying to anchor in the watery road.

All that remained was to wave them all a cheerful goodbye.

And then to enjoy—enjoy? to wallow in—the fruits of this labor.

J. Aubrey chuckled softly to himself and bent to fetch his thousands.

"Whitford!" a voice snarled from nearby.

He blinked. A voice? Calling him by name? Surely he had seen all his people aboard the lighter. He had counted them on quite carefully. Surely he hadn't missed any.

He straightened, looking into the face of a man he was sure he did not know. Not one of his expeditioners. Definitely not.

"You son of a bitch," this unknown man accused.

One corner of J. Aubrey's fine, full lips twitched, and he felt the beginnings of a tic flutter and thump at his right eye.

He tried on a bit of a smile.

The man before him scowled. "You son of a bitch," he repeated nastily.

Uh-oh, J. Aubrey thought.

FOUR

"YOU HAVE THE ADVANTAGE of me, sir." J. Aubrey was pleased to note that his voice did not tremble, despite the feelings that made his heart pound within. Who *was* this churlish fellow? An unknown quantity. A brigand? No, not in broad daylight. And not dressed so well. This man was of a better class than that of a common criminal. But so rude, so thoroughly unpleasant. And so large.

"Damn right I do," the man declared with obvious relish.

J. Aubrey was careful to control his eye movement. Do *not* look about. Never stare in the direction of the, um, exit. Of which, unfortunately, there was only one. The simple kiosk was crudely built from light lumber, a roofed enclosure with a half-wall at the front and a single small doorway to the left side. The man who now accosted J. Aubrey stood just to the left front of the structure. Entirely too close to that lone route of escape.

"Were you wanting passage on the *Yucatán Princess,* sir? I might yet be able to call her lighter back." The question was only mildly hopeful. This rude fellow did not have the appearance of a disgruntled gold-seeker any more than he looked like a snatchpurse or bullyboy.

J. Aubrey ventured a smile. It trembled only a little.

The gentleman before him barked. The sound of it was much too short and ugly for it to be considered a laugh. "You take me for a sucker, Whitford? Like one of those poor sons of bitches out on that boat?"

"Never," J. Aubrey assured him.

"Damn right I'm not," the large man swore with heat and feeling. "Gold discoveries indeed," he added. "You think I don't know who wrote those letters to the newspapers, Whitford? Well I do. I figured that out, you see. That's how I found you. You son of a bitch."

"I do wish you would refrain from using such language, sir," J. Aubrey said smoothly and with a smile.

Even as he spoke his brain was engaged in swift mental calculation.

The letters of announcement to the various New York newspapers had been prepared by J. Aubrey's own hand, of course. Although they were signed with other names, sealed with care and then scuffed as if to represent the passage of a long and difficult journey en route, with faked postmarks . . . everything done with the foresight and meticulousness of J. Aubrey's customary attention to detail.

The letters—they had to be the ones referred to—announced to the press a new discovery of gold deposits in distant Baja. The letters were essential to J. Aubrey's plan to mount an expedition.

But they had been prepared, he thought furiously, in private. Hadn't they? Almost in private, then. The only witness, so to speak, hadn't been interested in J. Aubrey's letter-writing. Not in the slightest. She had been . . .

J. Aubrey felt his heart leap and his stomach lurch.

The lady had been *married,* that was what she'd been.

And now . . .

"Mr. Cumberland, I assure you . . . it is Mr. Cumberland, is it not, sir? I assure you that, um . . ." He smiled as he spoke. Spread his hands wide in a show of innocence. Presented the unhappy gentleman with all the force of J. Aubrey's considerable charm.

"You son of a bitch," Cumberland snarled.

He started forward.

Toward, naturally, the only doorway in or out of the tiny kiosk.

Toward J. Aubrey Whitford.

And he held something—J. Aubrey couldn't see what—in his hand now. Something threatening. No doubt of that. A billy or knife or even a firearm? The precise nature of the threat scarcely mattered.

J. Aubrey felt faint. But he forced himself to wait. Forced himself to stand where he was and not to bolt in the obvious direction of safety. That was what Cumberland would be expecting.

He had to stand and wait until Cumberland passed behind the thin section of lumber, little more than a post really, that visually divided the openings of doorway and counter.

Only then would it be safe to make his move.

J. Aubrey stood sweating and tried to ignore the heart-thumping rush of blood in his ears. Tried to not feel the chill of icy sweat that suddenly beaded his broad and handsome forehead. Tried to control the tremors in his perfectly manicured fingers.

Three steps more. That was all he needed. Three steps. Now two.

He braced himself and planned in advance his each and every coming move.

The quick stoop downward. Grasp the handle of the case that sat at his feet. Lift and swing. First the case onto the counter. Then leap over the counter. Leap and roll. Swiftly to the feet again. Turn. Grab bag of hard-won gold coins. Eleven . . . thousand . . . wonderful . . . dollars. Grab. Spin. Run. Run where? No matter. Think about that when the time came.

Another step forward now. An eye-blink of time and Cumberland would be beyond view for half an instant. For time enough. It would *have* to be time enough. One more eye-blink and J. Aubrey could burst into flight.

He took a deep breath. Caught it inside his massively handsome chest and held it there.

Now!

FIVE

J. AUBREY'S HAND darted unerringly to the handle of the leather case. His knees bent just enough. Fingers found. Tightened. Grasped.

Straighten now. Lift. Lift and swing. Lift and . . .

He grunted.

He strained.

He *tried* to lift and swing.

Swing? He couldn't *lift.*

The case, weighted with more than eleven thousand cash dollars in gold and—curse the penny-pinchers who'd paid him thus —in silver too, was too damned heavy for J. Aubrey to snatch up to safety.

Run with it? Good Lord, he couldn't lift it off the *ground.*

J. Aubrey felt a scream rise into his throat and lodge there, gagging him.

The greatest, the finest, the most perfect scam in all the history of the game. And now this?

Never.

J. Aubrey Whitford's chest swelled with an indignant, defiant rage.

He spun to face the doorway.

Cumberland was there, damn his eyes.

The cuckold was there, all right.

But J. Aubrey Whitford was *here.*

And J. Aubrey Whitford was . . .

J. Aubrey Whitford was staring into the muzzles of the ugly little thing Cumberland held in his hairy fist.

J. Aubrey Whitford's rage turned to water.

That was a *gun* the man was holding.

One of those repeating things with a whole lot of tiny barrels arranged cylindrically about a common axis. The kind of firearm that could be fired over and over and over again without pause.

J. Aubrey Whitford knew, and cared, little about firearms.

But he knew a great deal about caution, thank you.

He blanched.

Yelped.

Ducked.

Cumberland shouted something. Extended his fist in J. Aubrey's direction. Yanked on the little dingus underneath the pistol.

There was a snapping discharge—not so loud as J. Aubrey would have expected, had he ever thought to anticipate such things—followed immediately by a most ugly slapping sound as something small and deadly smashed into the wooden kiosk wall over J. Aubrey's left shoulder.

J. Aubrey ducked—the movement was quite involuntary, actually—and while he was in the vicinity, tried a two-handed hold on the handle of his money bag.

Even that wouldn't do.

He couldn't lift the damned thing more than a few inches off the floor.

Cumberland was fumbling with the barrels of his gun. Trying to revolve another in line with the hammer?

"Don't!"

Cumberland ignored that heartfelt instruction, the man's concentration remaining on the item in his hands.

"No!"

Cumberland grunted. Straightened. Extended the pistol.

J. Aubrey Whitford abandoned all the fruits of his recent labors.

He sprang up. Out. Sailed over the vest-high countertop. Ducked his shoulder into a roll, but misjudged the distance to the wharf planking and landed heavily on his side. His head banged nastily against the planks, causing his ears to ring. The breath was driven out of him and his pain was intense. He'd probably be crippled for life, damn that Cumberland.

Cumberland leaned out over the counter. Aimed down at the man who lay practically at his feet.

All right, the pain wasn't all that intense nor the damage permanently crippling.

J. Aubrey shrieked and rolled aside as Cumberland discharged another barrel.

Once more there was that sickening sound of a leaden pellet thumping loudly into hard wood.

"I can explain!" J. Aubrey wailed as he came to his knees and then onto his feet.

Cumberland ignored him. Again began to fumble with the recalcitrant mechanism of his pocket-sized pepperbox revolving pistol.

J. Aubrey shook himself in an effort to clear the ringing from his ears. He looked wildly about as if for assistance. Although who might he turn to in such a desperate time as this? No one. He had no hope of rescue. His only resources were his own. His only assurance of safety was a matter of his own strength and cunning. J. Aubrey thought the situation through with care and clarity, if not with a great investment of time.

Cumberland, an *armed* Cumberland, stood inside the kiosk, virtually straddling J. Aubrey Whitford's eleven thousand dollar fortune.

Armed. That was the key to this question, was it not?

J. Aubrey shuddered.

Cumberland finished doing whatever he'd been doing with the firearm and extended his fist once more in J. Aubrey's direction.

Armed. Uh huh.

J. Aubrey turned his back on fortune, kiosk and cuckold alike, and began to run for his very life.

SIX

THERE WAS A SOUND behind him like that of a twig snapping. Big twig. *Real* brittle. Except this twig was a gunshot. J. Aubrey moaned a little and increased his speed all the more. Which he wouldn't have thought possible but managed to accomplish anyway.

Cumberland was back there shouting things. That was all right. Shouting was much better than shooting. Cumberland was also running, damn him. Chasing. J. Aubrey could hear the footsteps pounding on the planking of the quay. Keeping the pace right up, damn him. J. Aubrey felt a certain amount of indignation about that. If a lady was going to step out, dang her, a gentleman should be able to count on the injured party being elderly and fat and in no condition to conduct a foot race.

The footsteps behind slowed, and J. Aubrey began to smile even as he ran. That was more like it. Cumberland was flagging now.

A gunshot cracked another time. The smile disappeared from J. Aubrey's lips, as this time he heard the distinct and most unpleasantly intimate sound of a lead pellet sizzling past his left ear. Would that blasted gun never run out of bullets? The pace of the footsteps resumed speed. J. Aubrey groaned.

He raced down the crowded, cluttered wharf. Dodged past a sweating stevedore. Leaped over a bale of something-or-other. Caromed off the side of one up-ended keg, smashed into another and righted himself in a new direction of travel. Behind him Cumberland shouted something more, and a hand grabbed at J. Aubrey's flying coattails. "Make way. Make way." "Grab him. Stop that man!" "Make way there. Move aside." "Stop him."

J. Aubrey avoided the grasp of a sailor who tried to block his passage, then darted into the narrow gap between two towering piles of crates. This quay was *not* a suitable place for this sort of thing. Bundles and bales underfoot in all directions. Ships and sheer drops to one side. Warehouse walls to the other. He frowned and sprinted out from behind the crates, reversing direction as Cumberland tried to follow the path his quarry had just taken. J. Aubrey ducked underneath the boom of a cabled hoist and very nearly lost his hat. He grabbed it and pushed it down tighter onto his scalp, holding it there as he ran. Not his *hat,* dang it.

"Stop!"

J. Aubrey ran all the harder and all the faster.

Others along the East River wharf were taking up the hunt now, damn them. Jumping into the chase for the excitement of it. J. Aubrey'd never done anything to any of them. He was almost sure he hadn't.

If he could just lose Cumberland and those other mindless pursuers, damn them all, he could make it back to his kiosk before someone else discovered the bounty that'd been abandoned there. It made J. Aubrey ill to think of all that effort—and more to the point all that success—going to waste now.

Cumberland's gun fired again, and J. Aubrey found that event even more sickening than the thought of the bag of cash sitting forlorn on the kiosk floor. He ducked, even though he knew good and well that by then the reaction was ineffectively late.

"A hundred dollars to the man that catches him for me." Cumberland's voice came from farther away now. But there were other footsteps too now. More than ever.

Not fair, J. Aubrey protested. But only to himself. He didn't have breath to waste on complaint at this point. Not if Cumberland was being so unsporting as to offer a bounty, damn him. What sort of gentleman was this, anyway. If J. Aubrey only had a moment to discuss it with him. Reason with him. They could work it out quite nicely. J. Aubrey was sure of it. If only . . .

Some fleet-of-foot sailor boy ran close enough to take hold of J. Aubrey's right arm. J. Aubrey shook off the hand and veered aside. The sailor stayed with him, running stride for stride at his side, and trying to get a firm hold on J. Aubrey's sleeve.

"No, sir, you shall not." J. Aubrey hurdled a coil of rope and dashed between two casks. He heard a clatter and a grunt of pain. J. Aubrey permitted himself a small smile again.

If he could just pop out of sight now. A moment only. A few minutes at the very most. Then he could slip back to the kiosk, retrieve his possessions and be on his way. Just a very little while was all he asked. Just . . .

"There he is!"

J. Aubrey's pace had been slowing. His breath was laboring now, and there was a sharp stitch needling his side. He felt a sense . . . almost of despair . . . although it couldn't be that. J. Aubrey never despaired . . . never. And yet . . . He turned again and ran on in a clumsy, lumbering, laboring lope.

Shouts. Voices. Threats. Promises. Lordy!

He was becoming disoriented as well as tired. Where was that damned kiosk, anyway. Still ahead? Over to the right somewhere? He wasn't sure. And what would he do if he did manage to find it? Couldn't carry the money case, could he? Tried that already. Couldn't manage it even when he wasn't so tired. And why were these people still coming at him? Shouldn't they be giving up by now? They always gave up. For a hundred dollars? Would they wear a man's very life away for a measly hundred dollars in bounty blood money? Well, yes. Of course they would. And for eleven *thousand* dollars? For that much money a man could have half of New York razed and the other half depopulated.

The footsteps were coming closer now. Closer with every step. Close enough that he could hear the pursuers breathing.

J. Aubrey's legs were going. He felt limp and wobbly and knew he couldn't run much farther. His chest was heaving, and sweat soaked his shirt. For some reason he found himself hoping —foolishly, as he knew full well even as he continued to hope— that his shirt collar wouldn't become sweaty and go limp. It was the only collar he had remaining. Although what difference that would make if Cumberland caught up and shot a ball into his breast, J. Aubrey really didn't know. Seemed important at the time though. He heard a soft sound and realized the noise was his own and that he was whimpering between gasps.

The running men were nearly onto him now. Almost close enough to grab him and wrestle him down.

He angled left to avoid a pile of kegs. Stumbled over a taut cable and nearly fell. Grabbed for support at a piling. Righted himself and wobbled another few steps onward.

For some reason the sound of the footsteps behind had stopped now.

J. Aubrey staggered to a halt. Bent over, his chest was heaving and his legs trembling. He planted his palms on his knees and steadied himself, head down for a moment until he got a breath, then straightened and looked behind.

They were there all right. Half a dozen of them. Maybe more. He couldn't see for the piled kegs. At least half a dozen, though. Rough, ugly, rowdy-looking men. One of them held a bale hook in his fist. Another hefted a wood chunk, holding it upraised like a cudgel. They seemed in no hurry now.

"He's over here, mister." One of them motioned.

They were waiting for Cumberland to catch up, then. Waiting for the bounty money to be paid out before they turned J. Aubrey over to the man who wanted to murder him in cold, calculated blood.

"It's okay, mister. He ain't going anyplace now."

J. Aubrey looked behind him. And groaned. The wall of a ship's chandlery was built out onto the wharf here. The wall extended to the edge of it and a bit beyond, so lighters from the anchored ships could come and conveniently collect the chandlery's wares.

J. Aubrey was trapped in a pocket of open planking with the wall on one side, a virtual wall of kegs on another side, and a sheer drop to the filthy waters of the East River on the third side. The only opening to or from this trap was blocked by the grinning stevedores, several of whom were looking back toward Cumberland and motioning for the betrayed husband to hurry.

It seemed a bit late to be thinking about it, but J. Aubrey found himself wishing that he'd taken time somewhere along the way to gain instruction in the art . . . or was it a science . . . in the activity of swimming.

He stood beside the wharf edge and groped for a piling to support himself. He felt dizzy from the unpleasant combination of great exertion, intense stress and a severely limited intake of food in recent days. He felt, in fact, quite faint.

"Right here waitin' for you, mister. Now pay up an' he's yours."

J. Aubrey took his eyes off the cold, garbage-laden waters ten or more feet down and looked up to see Cumberland busily distributing coins into outstretched hands. J. Aubrey moaned.

Cumberland finished his business, gave J. Aubrey a look of triumph and reached into his coat pocket. The man pulled out the little pepperbox pistol and fumbled with it with both hands. They weren't a dozen feet apart here. And J. Aubrey had no place to run.

"So, Whitford. It comes to this," Cumberland told him. He sounded quite pleased about the thought. He satisfied himself with the mechanism of the pistol in his hands and raised it, taking careful aim on the center of J. Aubrey's chest.

Pride and honor required, of course, that J. Aubrey brace himself where he stood. Hold his chin high and his body still. That was the only correct way it could be done at this point.

J. Aubrey cleared his throat. He blinked. His vision was becoming quite fuzzy for some reason and perhaps a bit red-tinged as well.

He stared into the many muzzles of the little pistol. Into the cold, heartless eyes of the man who had come here to murder him.

If we could just talk about this for a moment, J. Aubrey wanted to say. He tried to speak, actually, but couldn't get the words to come out.

And now he wasn't conscious of being able to see anything. Not even those pistol muzzles. Not anything at all.

The red haze filmed his eyes and blinded him to all that was before him, and he felt a vague sense of weightlessness. But only for a moment.

J. Aubrey Whitford fainted dead away.

SEVEN

J. AUBREY WOKE to a dry mouth and a throbbing head. Those, however, were the very least of his worries.

He'd been shot. Quite seriously wounded. He could feel that all too well. The only puzzlement, really, was how he clung to this thread of life that remained his.

He'd been shot in the side. The right side. He could feel the bone-deep pain of it. And there was blood soaking his trousers from his knees downward. He could feel the chill dampness of the moisture as his own life's blood cooled in the humid atmosphere. He felt queasy, the combined effect of all his wounds making him feel as if he were rocking up and down, back and forth. He groaned aloud and wondered if he'd been left somewhere to die. Surely he had. Without doubt he was at this very moment engaged in the process of dying. With such a blood loss as he could feel soaking his lower self, he most assuredly must be nearly dead by now. "Jesus, Mary an' Joseph," he mumbled.

"Comin' around, are ye?" a voice responded.

"Pardon?" He hadn't actually been expecting an answer. Not unless he was already dead and unaware of the fact.

He blinked and found that he could see again now, although the only view available seemed to be that of clouds. Well, that figured, didn't it. They looked the same from the top, he noticed, as they had in life when seen from below.

"I said ye're comin' around now. Good."

J. Aubrey sat up, grunting with a certain amount of pain in his side.

He seemed to be in a small boat of some sort. Its rocking was the motion he'd felt. He was sprawled on the flooring at the back end of the thing, jammed tight on the floor with his head resting on the side of a crude seat.

There was a man seated on a board in the approximate center of the tiny craft. The man—a disreputable-looking sort with an unshaven face and unruly hair and yellowed, broken teeth—was surrounded by the accoutrements of a small watercraft. Oars. Ropes. Bundle of canvas. Long, thin staves of wood.

"I seem to be alive," J. Aubrey ventured.

"Mm," the man agreed. He grinned. "For the moment."

J. Aubrey looked down at his own side. It hurt, but he could not see any blood. Not even on his trousers, although they were indeed soaked with the moisture he'd felt upon first awakening. Water, he guessed now. It certainly wasn't blood.

"What, uh, happened?"

The man grinned again and reached into his coat pocket for a pipe and bit of tobacco. Took his time about loading the pipe and lighting it with the help of a burning glass that he produced from another pocket. "You dropped in on me, like."

"Do tell."

"Aye. I was tied up near Forester's Chandlery, see. Minding my own business whilst having a bite o' lunch, see. Heard this commotion above, an' then here you came. Dropped right down on top o' me, near. Landed half in an' half out my boat an' like to busted my gaff in two."

"Really."

"Aye, I said it, didn't I?"

"So you did," J. Aubrey said. He eyed the canvas-wrapped wooden bits that were laid in the small boat. He supposed one of them would be this gaff thing that he'd fallen onto. Probably that was why his side hurt so. But he hadn't been shot. That was the main thing, wasn't it. He smiled.

"Question now is, do I land you back t' that fella there, or do I not." The boatman motioned with his pipe stem toward the wharf.

J. Aubrey frowned. The wharf had been behind him, unnoticed until the boatman pointed it out. The small craft was standing off by fifty yards or so, floating in place in the East River.

Cumberland stood glaring out at them with his hands on his hips.

"Gentleman there offered me twelve dollars t' turn you over to him," the boatman said. "Thought I'd see if you got a better offer t' make afore I tell 'im aye or nay." The grin was back again. J. Aubrey was about to decide that he didn't particularly care for this man's grins.

"Twelve dollars, you say?"

"Aye. Twelve. Odd, eh? Tried t' bargain 'im up, but 'e wouldn't dicker. Twelve it is. Top dollar. Par'n me for sayin' so, mister, but you don't seem t' be worth all that much e'en if the fella does act distressed 'bout you bein' here. 'Twas my first impression that he was wantin' t' shoot you more'n twelve dollars worth."

J. Aubrey smiled. He was feeling good enough now to be able to do so with some confidence.

Why, he was alive, wasn't he? He had all his faculties, didn't he? No money, of course. But then his own native faculties were all the resource a gentleman of J. Aubrey Whitford's ingenuity should ever require. He sat up, tugged the slowly drying cloth of his pantlegs away from his skin and considered.

The simple truth was that J. Aubrey Whitford was worth a great deal more than twelve dollars to old Cumberland there. The man had already proven that. Had also, obviously, nearly exhausted his in-pocket resources when he paid that first bounty on J. Aubrey's head. Paid out everything except for twelve dollars in remaining cash. J. Aubrey barked out a short, happy laugh.

"Twelve dollars? My good man, I shall be pleased to present you with twenty-five dollars." J. Aubrey glanced toward the wharf where Cumberland waited. Boats are slow. Carriages and hacks are not. And there are eyes along every shoreline. J. Aubrey's smile firmed. "Paid upon my safe delivery aboard the good ship *Yucatán Princess,* sir, which I believe you can see yonder."

"Twenty-five dollars, you say?"

"In cash, sir. Twenty in gold and five in silver. If it matters."

"Can't say as it does," the boatman told him.

"Then we have a bargain, sir."

"Aye, we do." The man clamped his teeth, what few of them he had left, around the stem of his pipe and grinned that grin again.

"To the *Yucatán Princess* if you please, my good man."

"Take a bit o' time. Have t' rig sail an' work us out there. Won't catch yer ship 'til she heaves t' the pilot boat, I'd say."

"Perfectly all right," J. Aubrey assured him. "I am in no hurry now that I am in your excellent care, sir." J. Aubrey made himself comfortable on the stern thwart, as comfortable at least as was possible on such a hard and splintery bench. He folded his arms and pointedly ignored the arm-waving bluster that Cumberland was setting up a short distance away.

The boatman meanwhile was busy with nimble, practiced ease, stepping one of the wood pieces as a mast and running ropes and lines this way and that, until the rolled mess of canvas proved itself to be a sail, and the other wooden stave a thing to hold the top part of the sail higher than the short mast. Once the sail was up and filled with air, the boat began to heel and then to move on the choppy, dirty water. The gentleman named Cumberland receded slowly to insignificance as the boat, and J. Aubrey Whitford, sailed calmly away.

EIGHT

J. AUBREY would have been smiling, except for the fact that he was somewhat too busy for that at the moment. He was engaged in the serious business of holding to the gunwales of a small boat that leaned and jolted and shuddered quite alarmingly. Riding a small craft in a chop was *not* J. Aubrey's notion of fun and good times. The alternative, however . . .

"Can't you go any faster, Mr. Armbrister?"

The boatman gave him a disgusted look and spat over the downwind side of the boat. J. Aubrey took that to be a negative response.

The *Yucatán Princess,* sliding over the water with only a few of her canvas sails spread to the wind, was not moving particularly fast, yet Mr. Armbrister seemed unable to come alongside the much larger boat . . . ship . . . whichever. Armbrister, in fact, was zigging and zagging along behind at a lollygag pace.

"If you could just catch her, Mr. Armbrister, and put me aboard now . . ."

"Told you when we left, Mr. Whitford. That ship there, she won' closehaul 'til th' boat comes t' fetch the pilot off. An' that won' be 'til we reach the point." He pronounced it "pint" but fortunately pointed with an extended finger to show where he meant; otherwise J. Aubrey would have had no means of translation. "See there? Just off that pint, that's where she'll turn up t' the wind. Look ye there. That's the pilot boat now comin' off th' headland. See 'im?"

"I see him, but . . ."

"No but 'bout it, Mr. Whitford. That cap'n won' lose his way just 'cause o' my hail, an' I won' risk transferrin' ye without that ship lies to."

"That is kind of you, Mr. Armbrister. I appreciate your concern for my safety, but . . ."

Armbrister spat again and gave J. Aubrey a look this time that might have been pity. Pity for the ignorant? Possible. " 'Tain't the safety o' your bones that fret me, Mr. Whitford. 'Tis my boat here. That ship heels a tad more'n I calc'late, see, an' I'm dismasted or could be e'en worse. Twenny-five dollars gold an' silver won' buy me a new boat, Mr. Whitford. An' I won' take you alongside 'at ship 'til she lays to for the pilot boat."

"Of course, sir." J. Aubrey gave in to the inevitable as graciously as if the entire plan had been of his own making. He managed a smile and stared across the increasingly choppy water toward the craft that Armbrister said was the pilot boat.

He was not thinking, though, about ships or boats or transfers of personnel at sea.

Armbrister had mentioned the twenty-five-dollar fee that was owing on J. Aubrey's passage from the wharf to the *Princess*. Well, J. Aubrey hadn't honestly expected the fellow to let it slip his mind.

The question now was what to do about it.

J. Aubrey was unable to completely suppress the sigh that escaped his lips.

Eleven thousand dollars. Cash. Sigh. By now some light-fingered so-and-so would have discovered it. Stolen it. Such a terrible thing to do. Eleven thousand dollars was very nearly all the money there was in the world. A man who had eleven thousand dollars wouldn't even have to *think* about a paltry expenditure like twenty-five dollars.

But for a man who had only . . .

J. Aubrey sat silent at the back of the sailing boat and tried to conduct an inventory of his remaining assets. Without, that is, actually going through his pockets and making Mr. Armbrister question the wisdom of this journey, undertaken on the strength of promise alone.

He had the clothes he stood in—all right, sat in—with his chain and fob. He was cringing, and at the moment slightly queasy of belly due to all this bouncing, but no matter. He touched the front of his coat for reassurance. The slim, flat slab of the pen case was there. But then of course it was there. J. Aubrey would never part with that. The pen case left his person only when he was abed. And even then, only when he was alone. The pen case was essential to a gentleman of J. Aubrey's profession.

But as for his other possessions? They were few. A silk handkerchief tucked stylishly inside a sleeve. The skeletal key to a room he would not be able to return to.

As for actual money?

He had some large cent-pieces, carefully saved and carried in a front trouser pocket where they might jingle and show a bit of lump to any interested onlooker, implying more than their seven cents of worth. And he thought there might be a half-dime also. All right, then. Twelve cents in actual cash money.

Another sigh escaped J. Aubrey's lips.

Twelve cents was a poor fortune compared with eleven thousand dollars.

Hadn't he thought to slip *any* of that gold into a pocket rather than the bag?

He didn't think so, and more's the pity. Hadn't thought it necessary at the time, and of course one wants to make a show of being casual with and about the proceeds of the game. Damn!

All of it gone. Lost and . . .

He took firm control over himself. Gone was best forgotten. Brooding over losses was for losers. J. Aubrey preferred looking forward to pining behind.

He looked out toward the *Yucatán Princess* and the pilot boat that was approaching her. It couldn't be too terribly long now and he would make the transfer. The ship and two boats were coming together toward a single rendezvous point ahead.

Once that happened, why, matters should be simple enough.

Go aboard the *Princess* to, um, fetch the twenty-five-dollar passage fee back to Mr. Armbrister.

Transfer back off the *Princess* to the pilot boat. It was regretta-

ble, but he would have to secure passage on the strength of
promise once again.

Then back to shore with the pilot boat. New York, would that
be? Or Jersey? No matter. Once safely ashore and free of Cumberland—Armbrister too, of course; the fellow was sure to be
yelping and following, but that was the sort of thing that could
be sorted out when and as necessary—J. Aubrey would be able
to resume his, uh, activities.

Perhaps even another Baja expedition, eh? And why not.
There was still excitement stirring in the city, the Alta California
finds and great rush west not so very long ago. Those legitimate
tales remained active in the public consciousness. Now the Baja
California announcements generated by J. Aubrey himself.
Surely he could mount another, um, expedition westward. If not
to Baja (he wouldn't want that damned Cumberland tipped to
his whereabouts again), then—he stared ahead a moment more
—of course; then to Yucatán. That was somewhere close to the
Baja, was it not? Close enough. Exotic enough. Which is to say,
sufficiently unknown and mysterious to the gullible lads who
would want to travel there in search of yellow gold. Of course.
He could take his inspiration for this venture from the dear old
Yucatán Princess. Why not.

And this time, he thought with satisfaction, he would remember to offer package deals to his expedition members. Not
merely passage to this Yucatán place could be bought with their
fees—slightly increased fees, to be sure—but shovels, placer
pans, tents, clothing and foodstuffs too. Of course. A few crates
of genuine equipage. And rather more crates labeled but not
loaded. A tidy touch, that. And a tidy profit to boot.

J. Aubrey was able to smile despite his discomfort.

Cumberland had presented him with a small reversal and a
large challenge. But J. Aubrey Whitford remained, and was already at work. Everything beyond that was really of very slight
importance, after all.

He smiled again, and let go of the gunwales long enough to
rub his palms together in eager anticipation of the challenges to
come.

NINE

"WHY AREN'T YOU putting me onto the *Princess,* Armbrister? Get up there, man. Quickly now."

The boatman gave him another of those disgusted looks and spat. "Pilot boat's got th' right o' way. An' that 'ere ship's only got one boardin' ladder. Got t' wait our turn now they stopped."

"But the pilot boat . . ."

"Don't you fret y'self, Mr. Whitford. That pilot'll be clear in just a few minutes more. Then we can go a'side. They won' be leavin' ye behind."

J. Aubrey groaned. It was essential that he reach the ship before the other boat did. That damned pilot boat was his only way back to New York and fortune.

The *Yucatán Princess* was on its way to some godforsaken place down in the Floridas.

Didn't Armbrister understand? Of course he didn't. J. Aubrey felt a momentary pang of anger toward himself for forgetting that. Armbrister was being gulled out of the price of a passage and better *not* understand all that was going on here.

But if J. Aubrey failed to get aboard that pilot boat, failed to get back to the New York State shore . . .

The pilot boat crew knew their jobs and were not interested in lingering at the *Princess*'s ladder. The pilot boat drew alongside the *Yucatán Princess.* The man J. Aubrey presumed to be the harbor pilot was already scrambling down the rope ladder even while the boat was well astern of the larger ship, and barely needed to pause while the pilot dropped off the ladder and into the small boat.

Someone in the small craft barked a command, and a sailor used an oar to fend the boat away from the tall side of the

Princess. The man who'd just come down the ladder waved a perfunctory farewell to the expedition members who were lining the rail of the *Yucatán Princess,* and the pilot boat's crew rowed a little away from the side of the ship so they could gain wind that had been blocked by the hull of the larger craft. The small boat heeled and headed back for shore.

Without J. Aubrey Whitford aboard.

J. Aubrey shuddered and frowned.

"Now, Mr. Whitford, I can take you t' yer ship. An' I'll be thanking you, sir, t' pay me my twenny-five dollars now, if ye please."

"Of course, Mr. Armbrister. I consider it money well spent if I do say so."

"As I'd reckon ye should, considerin' what that gennelmun back there had in mind."

J. Aubrey gave Armbrister a reassuring smile and clutched tight to the gunwales, as the boat was maneuvered into position at the *Princess's* ladder.

Funny, he thought, how tiny and insignificant the *Yucatán Princess* had looked when she was riding to anchor in the East River.

Funny how immense and tall she looked from this water-level point of view.

He shuddered and—he was so rattled that he might even think of such a thing—briefly pondered whether he could talk Mr. Armbrister into returning him to New Jersey.

Without his pay, though, that damned fellow was sure to carry J. Aubrey not to Jersey but to Cumberland's waiting firearms. Armbrister had the look of a man who would be just vindictive enough to do such a thing.

J. Aubrey gave Armbrister a benign smile and waited patiently for the boarding ladder to come within reach.

I I

The Payoff

TEN

A HOST of eager hands reached down to J. Aubrey. Pulled him to the railing and over. The smiling members of the Baja expedition were pleased to see their leader aboard. But then they had never been privy to his alternate possibilities.

"Hey!" Armbrister barked from the seat of his little cockleshell boat far below. "You! What about m' damn pay for this trip?"

"Right," J. Aubrey said cheerfully. "I'm off to fetch it for you now." He turned and gave a wink to the several dozen men who counted on him to guide them to fortune. "That blackguard. We agreed on a fee for him to bring me out to you, then halfway here he tried to extort more from me. Can you believe the cheek of the man?"

There was a protective grumbling from the expeditioners, and several of the men leaned over the railing to send dark looks down at Armbrister.

"Naturally," J. Aubrey went on, "I pretended to go along with him. Couldn't miss out on our opportunities in the west, could I? No matter that I've been robbed ashore. I shall press on with you, gentlemen. Exactly as agreed." He smiled.

A few of the expeditioners began to look concerned now. "Robbed, you say?"

J. Aubrey was aware that soon enough someone would notice that he had come aboard without luggage, as well as having missed the pilot boat. Better to nip these little questions in the budding stage, he'd always thought. He continued to smile. "Ashore, as I said. Waylaid me at my lodgings when I went to collect my things. Got away with everything I had, damn them. But don't worry. I'd already stopped at the bank, gentlemen. Our expedition's funds are safe in bearer drafts." He smiled again and tapped his coat just below the lapel, as if referring to articles contained in the quite empty inside pocket there.

"But what about . . . ?"

"Could it wait, Mr. Harper? I believe the captain needs to get under way again, eh?"

A few of the men peered over the railing at Armbrister, who was setting up a most unseemly racket. J. Aubrey considered it a good thing that there were no ladies aboard. The boatman's language was unsuited for the ears of the fairer gender.

"What d' you want us to do about him, Mr. Whitford?"

"Ignore him, Mr. Faust. I daresay he'll not pursue us all the way to the Baja."

"We could knock him in the head for you if you like," the expeditioner offered.

"Don't bother yourself, please."

"You're a generous man, Mr. Whitford. Kindly to a fault, I say, what with the way that man tried to do you."

"Live and let be is my motto, Mr. Faust. I shan't exercise myself over the likes of him."

The men of the expedition gave their leader looks of glowing approval, while J. Aubrey made his way rearward along the deck of the *Yucatán Princess* to assure Capt. Baker that they could now proceed.

Not that J. Aubrey had much choice about going forward now. The pilot boat was long gone, and Armbrister was a most unlikely source of transportation back to shore.

J. Aubrey would simply have to travel with the Baja-bound group.

As far, at least, as the next landfall.

He adjusted the set of his handsome silk hat and made his way with considerable dignity toward the steering area, whatever it was called, where the captain and several other men stood.

ELEVEN

J. AUBREY'S NOSE wrinkled. His lip curled. This was so . . .
distasteful. So . . . undignified.

He made a face, then resigned himself to the inevitable and
picked up the offensive article, lifting it with the tips of thumb
and forefinger only, touching it as little as possible.

He sighed.

There simply wasn't any help for it, was there.

He stepped into the donated cotton balbriggans. Then into
the donated cotton—*cotton!* good Lord—breeches. Finally he
shrugged the donated, and quite frayed, striped jersey over his
handsome head and down past his chest and shoulders.

His nose wrinkled again. He couldn't help it. He looked like
a *sailor.* Like an oaf was more like it. J. Aubrey groaned aloud
and tried to put the best possible face on things.

The donated articles of clothing were clean, after all.

They didn't reek of stale perspiration.

They didn't . . . they didn't at all suit him, that was what
they didn't.

He sighed once more.

If he could only have had a *bath* before changing.

Capt. Baker, damn him, hadn't budged on the subject, despite
J. Aubrey's fervent appeals.

Couldn't use up the fresh water, Baker'd said. Not even
enough for a sponge bath, Baker'd said. Feel free t' use all the
salt you want, Baker'd said.

J. Aubrey scowled. He'd *tried* bathing in salt water already,
thank you. The experience was not one he would willingly re-
peat.

But after five days afloat, a man simply had no choice. Fresh
garments were a necessity at such times.

Thinking about that made J. Aubrey think about Baker again. And consequently scowl again.

Damn Baker anyway. Wouldn't put into port and let a man off, no matter the passionate entreaties. Wouldn't make landfall again until Augustine, Baker declared. Wouldn't listen to sweet reason, J. Aubrey interpreted. Wouldn't allow a man to get on with things.

No, thanks to that miserable Baker, J. Aubrey Whitford was trapped aboard a stupid, floating pesthole, along with more than a score of dupes too dumb to know they'd been fleeced.

Trapped, damn it.

And probably back in New York some tinhorn scammer was happily riding the coattails of J. Aubrey Whitford's brilliance. Probably by now there were half a dozen gamesmen—of lesser foresight and capability than J. Aubrey Whitford—who right this moment were busily engaged in reaping rewards from the seeds J. Aubrey'd sewn. Mounting their own expeditions to the Baja on the strength of J. Aubrey's carefully planned announcements. Shearing sheep who rightfully belonged to J. Aubrey.

The mere thought of it was enough to make a man ill.

J. Aubrey's gorge rose, wedging tight into his throat, and he did indeed feel quite ill.

Not, however, that the physical illness had anything to do with the distress of his current disappointment. It had to do, rather, with yet another change of course that set the picayune *Princess* to wallowing across the waves.

Why couldn't Baker settle on a smooth, placid, motion-free course and hold to it?

J. Aubrey tried to fight off the seasickness. Tried to ignore the sweaty, heaving biliousness that roiled his stomach and weakened his knees.

After all, he couldn't expel from his belly food that he hadn't eaten, could he? And he hadn't eaten anything in quite some time now.

He thought about this with calm reason.

And then bolted for the passageway and the lee railing—oh, he'd learned about upwind and down, all right—beyond.

He draped himself miserably over the rail, paid sad penance there for ten minutes or so, then shakily staggered forward—the front was forward, the back was aft; he was becoming quite nautical in his terminology lately—to find a seat on a bale of deck cargo. The other members of the expedition saw their leader's plight and were considerate enough to grant him his privacy.

J. Aubrey sighed and wiped his mouth with the tail of his shirt. That was one advantage of having to wear rags, he supposed. The norms of attire no longer applied.

He sighed and . . . and blinked.

Realized what he'd been doing and firmed his chin. Feeling mawkishly sorry for himself, that was what he'd been doing ever since he discovered he wouldn't be allowed ashore ahead of the expedition party.

But was J. Aubrey Whitford defeated? Never! Was J. Aubrey Whitford depressed? Only temporarily, by damn.

Circumstances might knock him down.

Nothing would be permitted to keep him there.

J. Aubrey held his head up. Peered infinitely far ahead of the wallowing *Yucatán Princess*.

Down, sir, was far from out. Down was only opportunity in disguise.

If Baker would not land him apart from the expeditioners, why, he would simply have to press on and make the most of things. Create opportunities where none seemed to exist. Of course. He grunted in contemplation. The members of his expedition wouldn't have paid over *everything* to their leader for the privilege of joining. They had been asked only for a set price of passage. Why, there was no telling how much additional cash these worthy gentlemen carried with them. For contingencies. And one of the finer qualities of the domestic sheep is that it can be sheared over and over again.

How far was it to this Augustine place, anyway? Some days?

Why, that would be barely enough time for J. Aubrey to prepare. And a gentleman must always be prepared to meet a challenge.

For the first time in days, J. Aubrey Whitford smiled.

He thought about the pen case residing still in his coat pocket down in the pestilential quarters he'd been given.

No matter about that, though. The important thing was that he still had his pen nibs. Ink? A bit, he thought. If the ink powder hadn't been ruined by the humidity and salt air.

He would need paper, of course, and in appropriate sizes. Parchment would be best. Baker might be able to supply something suitable. Or even one of the expedition members. The oddities those men had thought to haul with them . . .

Pens, ink, parchment he would need. And time. Lots of time. A steady writing surface, of course. That could present something of a problem while aboard. Hours of work could be destroyed by a single mis-stroke if the ship wallowed and jolted at an inconvenient moment.

No matter. He would cope. He had a plan now, did he not? All he needed more was to execute that plan.

And for that, J. Aubrey required only his own inner resources and a bit of time to implement it all.

He sat with shoulders squared and eyes toward the horizon, and thought about how he might best go about turning disaster into gold.

TWELVE

J. AUBREY SMILED as Harry Field stopped beside him and leaned onto the rail, with his weight on his elbows and his hands clasped. Both men looked across the gray-green water toward a heavily wooded shore. The shoreline seemed quite foreign and exotic in appearance. It lay flat and furry in the distance, the emerald-hued growth near its banks unnaturally dense, and the background innocent of mountains or even hills. Some of the trees looked like bare sticks with puffs of odd, elongated greenery at their tops. The trees that looked like ordinary trees appeared to be shrouded in a pale gray mist, despite the heat of the midday sun.

"Strange country, Mr. Whitford," Field observed.

"Yes."

"Dif'rent."

"Yes."

"But this ain't the Baja itself, right?"

"Right," J. Aubrey willingly agreed. "To hold our expedition costs low, you see, I contracted with Capt. Baker to bring us this far. The port is called St. Augustine. The fort . . . can you see it there? . . . is Marion." The tall, pale walls were barely visible across the water to the south. "Used to be Castle Saint Marcos. Something like that. Spanish, anyway."

Field seemed eager now. Spanish, the expedition leader had said. And therefore, obviously, close to the Baja, where the great new gold fields had been discovered. As reported in all the major newspapers. Field, J. Aubrey had discerned over the course of the voyage, was one of the more outspoken members of the expedition. Convince Harry Field of something and all the others would fall meekly into line.

And fortunately neither Field nor anyone else in the group

knew much about geography south of, say, New Jersey. J. Aubrey had been *very* careful to determine that much about them.

"It would take a passage around the Cape for us to sail direct to the Baja, Mr. Field. That would be much too time-consuming as well as too expensive. Can't have others beating us to the gold claims, can we now, ha ha?"

"Cape, Mr. Whitford?"

"Cape," J. Aubrey confirmed. "Horn, Hope, whichever one it is. Underneath South America, anyway. Very long way around. We can't waste that amount of time just for the convenience of riding comfortable in a ship while we travel."

"Of course not." Field smiled and stood upright, bending backward at the hips to ease his back before resuming his place on the rail. Several of the other expeditions drifted to them and clustered about.

"We go overland from here, right?" Field asked.

"Right. We disembark here with all our equipment, then overland to the Baja."

"Will there be wagons provided?" someone asked.

"I contracted for wagons to meet us, yes," J. Aubrey replied with a glib and easy smile.

Wagons? Good Lord. These men must think they're off on a jaunt to the wilds of Lake Erie or something. Wagons indeed. The poor saps didn't realize they were barely on the same continent as this Baja place once they disembarked at St. Augustine. J. Aubrey didn't know much about Baja and knew less about the Floridas, but at least he knew they were not exactly close neighbors.

"How long before we reach the gold fields, Mr. Whitford?" Bolliger asked.

"That all depends on the conditions in the . . . conditions of the road, sir." He'd been about to say something about conditions in the mountains. After all, everyone knew, more or less, that gold was supposed to be found in association with mountains. But there didn't seem to be much in the way of mountains in view down here. Better not to raise that question, he'd realized barely in time.

"Within a few weeks, would you say?" Bolliger persisted.

"It all depends, doesn't it, on how we perform along the way." J. Aubrey smiled. That was better. Put the onus where it belonged. On someone else.

"In that case," Field declared, "we'll be there in a matter of days."

"Good," J. Aubrey chortled, slapping Field on his meaty shoulder. "Good for you, Harry. That's the spirit I like to see. That's the spirit that will make you a rich man before this is over." Or me, J. Aubrey added quite to himself. No, this game wasn't over yet. Not by a long shot. These fellows still had coins in their purses. And J. Aubrey intended to do them each the kindness of allowing them to walk lighter on their feet by relieving them of all that weight.

"We'd best clear away from the deck and go below. We need to see to our gear," J. Aubrey suggested, "and the crew will be busy here when we come into port."

Ah, there was eagerness indeed in all these faces now. J. Aubrey was genuinely pleased to see that. "Step lively now," he said, a locution he'd picked up aboard the tubby little ship. "It's off to the Baja for us, gentlemen."

THIRTEEN

ST. AUGUSTINE was interesting enough, as ports went. And certainly exotic enough to satisfy the sense of wonder that J. Aubrey could see in his expeditioners' eyes as they stood transfixed on the odd, stone quay and stared about them.

The very stone the wharf was built of seemed exotic. It looked and felt something like limestone, yet seemed to be made of countless tiny seashells compacted and joined somehow together.

The foliage around them was even more exotic. Lush, flowery plants. Spiky cactuses. Tall palm trees that clacked and clattered in the onshore breeze. And in the few oaks, a lacy gray stuff that hung like rags from the branches and was called moss, although it looked nothing at all like the soft and fuzzy green mosses of the north.

Lying just north of the tropical harbor, and commanding it with its cannon was the Castillo de San Marcos, lately Fort Marion, with its rounded sentry towers and jack-o'-lantern-toothed gun embrasures along the upper walls.

It seemed almost odd to see the good old Stars and Stripes flying from the flagpole over the fort.

The residents of the sleepy little port town made up for that, though. They were for the most part dark-complected and dark-haired, and the conversations heard along the quay were more often undertaken in Spanish than not. J. Aubrey approved of that little touch of unexpected verisimilitude.

The *Yucatán Princess* had been able to tie up directly to the quay here—there certainly wasn't any other competing traffic to interfere—and the process of off-loading had taken barely any time at all. Already Capt. Baker and crew were warping the *Princess* away and preparing to sail somewhere or other.

J. Aubrey and his people crowded together beside their piles of crated, boxed and bagged equipment.

"Shouldn't there be someone here to, um, meet us?" expeditioner Daniel Warren asked timidly.

"Certainly," J. Aubrey assured him with a broad smile. He glanced around, making sure he had the attention of one and all. He did. Without doubt he certainly did. "Can you all hear me? Yes?" He waited for the responding nods before he proceeded.

"My factor should be here to greet us at any time now. I've arranged with him for our temporary quarters in St. Augustine and for our wagon transportation westward. Everything all arranged and paid for before we ever left New York, gentlemen, so have no fear. Be patient with me a little longer, and we shall soon be on our way. I know Mr. McKenzie will be along direct he hears of our arrival."

J. Aubrey motioned as if to pluck his watch out, then remembered in time that he had none and turned the gesture into one of smoothing down his lapel. Lordy, but it felt good to be back in proper attire once more. Having to wear borrowed clothing while aboard the *Princess* had been a trial. Now, thank goodness, he felt himself again.

"This man McKenzie is to meet us here?" Junius Hankins asked. Stupidly, in J. Aubrey's opinion; he'd just said as much, hadn't he?

J. Aubrey, however, was accustomed to dealing with the stupid, the foolish and the inept. Bless them. He counted on most men to fall into one or more of those categories. How else could an entrepreneur expect to make a living?

J Aubrey responded with the sort of smile that implies that his questioner has just brought up the most critically sensible of all possible questions. "Exactly, Mr. Hankins. All arranged well ahead of time. Although naturally I could not be specific with McKenzie about our date of arrival. The uncertainties of sail and all that. But he is expecting us, oh yes. Once he hears that the *Yucatán Princess* has made port, Mr. Hankins, I am sure he will rush into action on our behalf. No question about it." J. Aubrey's smile remained undiminished.

McKenzie. J. Aubrey'd actually known a McKenzie once. And a nasty sort he'd been, too. Pimple-faced, overgrown bully. But all that had been a good many years ago. J. Aubrey'd grown up since then. Wherever that McKenzie was, whatever might have become of him since he left the neighborhood those many years ago, J. Aubrey Whitford still wished the mean, hard-fisted bugger ill. In fact, J. Aubrey quite often used the name McKenzie when he wanted to invent a party to lay blame upon.

Ever since he was forced to leave New York, J. Aubrey'd been playing this one quite by ear.

He gave his Baja gentlemen a benign smile, though, and settled himself on a crate that was marked as the property of W. Smith. He crossed his legs, squared his freshly brushed silk hat and wished he had a cane to add to the pose. A cane can be just the finishing touch a gentleman needs. Perhaps J. Aubrey should acquire one soon. There would be a way to do that, he expected. Something should come to mind soon. He folded his hands on his own lap in lieu of having a cane to lean upon, and went about the business of waiting patiently, calmly, comfortably for a man named McKenzie to show up and collect them.

FOURTEEN

"WHAT DO YOU MEAN you don't know McKenzie? Of course you know McKenzie. You simply must. This isn't that large a community after all, sir. Why, I've corresponded with the man here. Advanced him a great deal of money toward this enterprise, in fact." J. Aubrey appeared shocked. Amazed. Concerned. His features could be quite expressive when he desired. The Baja expeditioners gathered close around, while J. Aubrey interrogated the local resident—at the expeditioners' insistence —once dusk made it clear there would be no McKenzie-sent wagons today.

J. Aubrey wrung his hands in consternation. Exclaimed. Protested. Reiterated. All to no avail. The gentleman from St. Augustine did not know any McKenzie.

"But he is our factor here. I've already paid him, you see, to arrange for our lodging here and transportation across the isthmus to the Baja."

"Isthmus? What the hell isthmus is that supposed to be?" the local demanded.

It was all J. Aubrey could do to keep himself from smiling. Thank goodness. A local with some knowledge of geography. Perfect. In addition to everything else, this would save J. Aubrey from having to admit to any knowledge that they were on the wrong continent. So to speak.

"This isthmus, of course. We are to travel from here to the Baja," J. Aubrey said with a show of confidence. "Across to the Baja where the new . . . well, never mind, sir, why it is we need to go there. Suffice it to say that we are en route to this Baja. Mr. McKenzie arranged for all our needs once we reached your lovely community."

The gentleman, who had the look of a seafarer about him,

chuckled and shook his head. "Mister, you been flimflammed. You've all been had."

"Sir?"

"This Baja? I've heard of it. It's on the other side of Mexico."

"Certainly," J. Aubrey agreed.

"This here is Florida, mister. Not Mexico."

"But . . ."

"Not even close to being Mexico, you see."

"This Baja place you want to get to, first you got to go to the other side of Florida. Then all the way across the Gulf of Mexico. *Then* you can head out to the Baja. But, Lordy, mister, you must be two thousand miles from it yet. Maybe more'n that."

J. Aubrey reeled. He was aghast. He was in a state of shock. How could this be? And he had *trusted* Mr. McKenzie. Advanced him a large sum of money. Out of J. Aubrey's own pocket. It was all to have been arranged. Now, sir, he was to understand that he had been *bilked?* Ah, such devastation. J. Aubrey could scarcely believe it. He had trusted McKenzie. And now this? What was the world coming to if a gentleman's word was of no value? J. Aubrey avoided sobbing aloud. But barely.

The expeditioners crowded close around. Their sympathies, naturally, lay with J. Aubrey who was their own known and trusted—and now betrayed—leader. They were too concerned over this damned McKenzie's thievery and deception of a trusting Mr. Whitford to think of placing any blame on the innocent leader of their Baja venture. The nerve of that fellow. People like McKenzie should be locked up.

"Do you happen to know, sir," a sad and chastened J. Aubrey meekly inquired, "of somewhere we could put up for the night? Until we . . . work this out? And, uh, are you quite *sure* you don't know McKenzie?"

Several of the expeditioners went so far as to comfort J. Aubrey with pats on the shoulder, and with hard looks at the somehow offending local gentleman who was the bearer of these bad tidings.

J. Aubrey had some small amount of difficulty in maintaining a straight face.

FIFTEEN

J. AUBREY felt quite content as he walked outside in search of a little solitude. He found a piling to sit on and settled onto it happily, crossing his ankles and peering off across the dark waters of the Atlantic.

He really couldn't ask for much better than this. It was all falling so nicely into place.

The good folk of St. Augustine had been quite properly appalled to hear that someone flying false colors brought these Baja pilgrims to their doorstep.

The owner of a dockside warehouse offered unused space where the travelers could store their equipment and spread their blankets.

The ladies of the town provided a most toothsome potluck dinner attended by strangers and locals alike. A trifle heavy on seafood dishes, J. Aubrey thought, but tasty nonetheless. And with heartfelt good fellowship shared by townspeople and passers-through, the disparate groups became acquainted.

Sympathies were expressed. Hands were shaken. Oh, it was wonderful the way people banded together to assist unfortunates in times of distress.

J. Aubrey smiled. Why, he hadn't even had to do much in the way of guiding the conversations that took place among his expeditioners afterward. It was all following the delightfully predictable pattern he desired.

The expeditioners "knew" that Mr. Whitford had been bilked, through no fault of his own of course, by that dastard McKenzie.

A few were already proposing that the expedition members pitch in to make good the losses suffered because of McKenzie.

J. Aubrey's smile grew broader.

Naturally the good Mr. Whitford declined the tentatively suggested offer of financial support.

The smile became quite broad indeed.

He declined the suggestion tonight because some member of the group was sure to remember that Mr. Whitford was supposed to be carrying bank drafts of eleven thousand or so dollars.

Another disaster or two, though . . .

He heard footsteps on the stone behind him—the locals called the odd stuff *coquina*—and turned to see who was coming. Warren, he thought.

"Good evening, Daniel."

"I'm not bothering you am I, Mr. Whitford?"

"Not at all, Daniel. I'm pleased for the company," J. Aubrey politely stood. There was no piling close by on which to offer a seat.

"I hope you didn't think I was out of line back there. Um, suggesting that we reimburse you for the losses you suffered."

"It was considerate of you, Daniel. I appreciate it. But of course I cannot accept. The choice of that man as our factor was mine alone. I accept full responsibility for my error."

"You're a good man, Mr. Whitford. We're lucky to have you to guide us."

"Believe me, Daniel, I shall try to do better in the future."

"I, we that is, just wanted you to know that you have our full confidence, Mr. Whitford. What happened here, it wasn't your fault. We can see how it's affected you. How much you care about all of us. It's a shame, that's what it is, Mr. Whitford. Robbed in New York, now cheated by your own man here. But we want you to know that we're foursquare behind you. All of us are."

"Thank you, Daniel. I appreciate that." J. Aubrey meant every word of that, too. Appreciated it? He was counting on it.

"Yes, well . . ." Warren stood awkwardly before J. Aubrey for a moment, hemming and hawing and staring toward the toes of his shoes. "Yes," he repeated.

"Thank you, Daniel. I thank all of you. You are a fine group of men. I only wish . . ."

"None of that, sir. It wasn't your fault. We know that." Warren cleared his throat, fidgeted a moment longer, and then turned and bolted back toward the warehouse that was the expedition's temporary—and free—quarters in St. Augustine.

J. Aubrey watched the little man go and sent a small, fond smile toward Daniel Warren's back. Bless him and all the beloved sheep who were like him.

He turned back once more to enjoy for a moment longer the black emptiness of the vast ocean and the feel of the night breeze on his cheeks. The air smelt of salt and of freedom, and not far away he could hear the gentle clatter of palm fronds rattling in the wind. At times like this J. Aubrey felt he owned the whole of the wide, wonderful world. Or very soon would.

He gave his flock time enough to talk privately among themselves a bit longer, time enough for them to seek the comforts of sleep after so trying a day, then made his way back to the warehouse to join them.

He made only one brief detour on his way to his own borrowed bedding.

The door to the warehouse offices, he'd already ascertained, was closed and latched but not actually locked. It was, J. Aubrey reflected, a most considerate habit.

SIXTEEN

"COULD I BORROW paper and ink, Mr. Merriwether, and perhaps the use of your office? I need to warn my associates in New York about McKenzie's crimes."

"Of course, Mr. Whitford. Glad to be of help," the St. Augustine warehouse owner said. "Anything we can do, right?"

"You are too kind, sir. Too kind to us, indeed." J. Aubrey smiled and bowed low to the stocky, middle-aged man whose hospitality the entire group was enjoying.

"Them friends of yours back in New York ain't gonna get us out of this pickle," the man who called himself Smith growled.

"No, they will not," J. Aubrey agreed readily. "But I consider it only decent and proper to warn them nonetheless."

Smith grunted and turned away, and J. Aubrey moved off in the direction of Merriwether's office. He already knew the way. Rather better, in fact, than the good Mr. Merriwether might have wished.

J. Aubrey supposed he would have to waste some time scrawling a letter and addressing it to someone in New York, just to make this look good. Not that he cared a fig what happened to anyone there at the moment. And not that there really was a McKenzie to warn anyone against.

Still, appearances must be maintained. He'd said he wanted to write a letter, therefore a letter there must be.

What he needed in truth was the ink that he hadn't been able to find last night. His own ink powder had become hardened and unusable aboard ship, drat it. Otherwise he'd have had much of his work already done on this.

He gave Merriwether a genial smile and effusive thanks when the man produced the items J. Aubrey needed—whoever would have thought to look for ink *there,* anyway—and handed over a sheaf of paper and several pre-formed, pre-glued envelopes as well. Most helpful of him, to be sure. Most convenient.

"I'll leave you alone now, Mr. Whitford."

"Thank you, Mr. Merriwether. Thank you for everything."

J. Aubrey settled himself at Merriwether's big rolltop and took his time preparing.

He was, after all, a craftsman.

He removed his coat and rolled his shirt-sleeves. Laid his pen case down in precisely the most comfortable position, fidgeting and adjusting it several times before he was satisfied. Shot his jaw and rolled his head in slow circles to relieve tension in the neck. Stretched his arms and flexed his fingers. Mmm, it all felt fine. Fine indeed.

He prepared an ordinary ink first, adding only a bit of water to the powder to get a simple writing consistency. He tested the ink with a few scrawled lines and an everyday pen nib first. That piece of paper would serve as the "letter" he would post to New York. No one would open the envelope once sealed, and there was enough ink on the page to show through if anyone should hold the envelope to the light. A man didn't want to take chances with such things. One simply never knew.

He began to jot down a make-believe address, then laughed and addressed his envelope to Mrs. Cumberland. Wouldn't *that* make Mr. Cumberland furious. And would the fellow ever believe there was no meaning to the chicken-scratchings on the page? Ha! Never.

J. Aubrey chortled happily for a moment, then became serious once again.

A serene outlook was what was needed here. Calm and an expert hand. Mmm.

He swirled his pen through the ink he'd made, pondering the consistency for a moment. His judgment here was critical.

A touch more ink powder, he thought. He used the tip of one of the smaller nibs to lift a minuscule amount of powder out of the jar and dropped it into the black fluid already created. More again? Not yet, he decided. Thick was good but not *too* thick.

He stirred the mixture with the flat steel nib he'd used to address the "letter" that would enrage that no-account Cumberland.

Not bad.

Now . . .

He fetched down the oil lamp that sat on top of Merriwether's desk. Unscrewed the filler cap. Dipped the steel nib in and extracted a drop of whale oil. Swirled it into his ink. A touch more oil, he thought. Good. He stirred. And smiled.

It was *so* difficult to get just the right sheen once the ink dried. Practically no one understood the difference between seeing a handwritten ink and a printed ink. But practically everyone can see that difference once the ink has dried on paper.

The secret to J. Aubrey Whitford's successes was—among many other things too, of course—that he did understand these differences.

Once J. Aubrey was done forging a document, why, anyone, everyone would accept it as printed, not written.

He smiled again.

The oil seemed just right. Now a bit of graphite. He pulled a pencil from his pocket—obtained the previous night just in case he hadn't managed to secure the use of the office here—and used the side of the steel pen nib to shave a small amount off the lead. Perfect, J. Aubrey congratulated himself. Wonderful.

He stirred his ink again and tested it on a scrap of waste paper. He wouldn't be sure until it dried, of course, but he thought he was already close to what he wanted here.

He looked fondly at the case of gold foil pen nibs—real gold too, no substitutes would do for this; these gold pens were his most treasured possessions, the tools of his best labors. Now he could begin the task of creating a set of printed bank drafts complete with seals and emblems, naturally with dates and amounts and authorizing signatures all hand-written. He would have to make up a new and ordinary batch of ink for that, of course. Paler and lightly tinged with a shade of violet. And he'd go back to the steel pen tip as well.

But for the "printed" draft forms, nothing but his gold nibs and his own exceptional calligraphic abilities would do.

J. Aubrey was genuinely happy as he bent to his task. He could already see in his mind's eye the intricate detailing he would have to create here. Could already visualize the final documents looking as if they had just rolled off a printer's platen.

He began to hum a gay tune under his breath, completely unaware that he was doing so, as he fitted into his pen barrel the first of the many nibs he would require. He flexed his shoulder muscles one final time and then bent over the sheet of silk bond —infinitely richer than the plain foolscap Merriwether had offered him—that he'd appropriated last night.

SEVENTEEN

J. AUBREY let them think of it first. Of course. Things always worked out more agreeably if the ideas came from someone else.

"We have to find a way to go on. We can't come this far only to turn our backs with fortune practically in our grasp." It was Haywood Bolliger speaking, once a hatter and more recently an apothecary. A failed hatter and a failed apothecary to be sure. J. Aubrey had overheard poor Bolliger's conversations while they were at sea. Quite naturally the man never admitted to his failures in either trade. But why else would he now be seeking gold in a distant land, mmm? Bolliger, like all of them, was a failure who sought the services of another to lead him to fortune. And who was thoroughly committed now to this journey. In for a penny, in for a pound. So predictable. J. Aubrey hid a small smile behind his fist.

"I say we hire another ship," Bolliger declared. "I say we go on exactly as planned."

"Exactly as planned? We can't go on as planned," a limp and perspiring Thomas Lancaster injected. "That damned McKenzie has already stolen our funds, remember. We have nothing to go on with."

"Nonsense. We all have some reserves left. We can . . ."

"No," J. Aubrey said in a voice that was sharp despite its soft volume. He'd been hanging back. Now he stepped into the middle of the group. "I cannot allow you gentlemen to suffer for my failings. I should have seen that McKenzie was a hoodwink. That responsibility must be mine alone." Better he point it out himself than allow others—the man who called himself Smith for instance—to whisper it behind his back.

"My profits may be gone, but I have some savings, you know.

I am not without resources." He turned to their St. Augustine benefactor Merriwether, who seemed to have adopted a mother hen attitude toward the stranded travelers. "Mr. Bolliger is correct, sir. These gentlemen are entitled to the completion of our enterprise. Do you know if a ship can be found?"

Merriwether fingered his chin, kneading the taut skin of his jaw as if hopeful of reshaping it to a more comely appearance. "None to the isthmus, Mr. Whitford. Not from here. Might find something out of Cuba if you could get that far. But I don't know of any ships to Cuba either. Know of one captain who calls here occasionally New Providence bound. You might convince him to carry your people. Hope to find another to Cuba and something from there to the isthmus for the crossing to the Pacific."

Bolliger and some of the others began to look hopeful. "Would that take long?" someone asked eagerly.

"Oh, I dunno," Merriwether said. "I know of a ship that should be stopping here next month or thereabouts. That would get you across to New Providence. From there . . . ?" He shrugged. "Three months total. If things work out well for you. Twice, three times that otherwise."

The expeditioners' faces fell.

"Surely, sir, there must be a better way," J. Aubrey put in. "It cannot be a secret now why we wish to reach the Baja. There are new gold discoveries there, Mr. Merriwether. We must be among the first to reach the gold fields or all our efforts will be for naught."

"I dunno." Merriwether rearranged his face again. The sad thing about that was that the flesh always returned to its original shape once he was done with it. "Way I understand it, gentlemen, this Baja is t'other side of Mexico."

"Yes, indeed." All the expeditioners agreed about that now. They had taken considerable pains to acquaint themselves with the geography of the tropics after their arrival in St. Augustine.

"I know a ship leaving for Texas," Merriwether suggested. "Captained by a friend of mine, in fact. And Texas is smack next to Mexico. If you could get to Texas, why, you could walk the rest of the way to your Baja. It can't be so terrible far once you get to Texas."

The expeditioners' interest quickened. Except, that is, for J. Aubrey's. His intentions required a certain amount of difficulty in securing transportation. And a certain amount of need for financing that transportation. How else could he hope to extract a fair share of cash from the expedition members.

"Mmm, I suppose you could take ship from here to Texas," Merriwether went on. "I could help arrange that. But there would be passage fees. You have to understand that. Even though the captain of this ship is a friend of mine, I couldn't ask him to take on passengers without the payment of some small fees."

"We'll do it," Bolliger said firmly.

"We haven't the money to do it," Lancaster said.

J. Aubrey knew better than to seek excuses for delay on a shore so impossibly distant from the Baja. One suspicious mood swing and all his hope for future profits would evaporate. "I can pay," he said quickly. "I will pay passage for all of us if Mr. Merriwether will be kind enough to intercede for us with his captain friend."

Even Smith and his cronies smiled.

"To Texas," someone yelped, lamely trying to begin a rallying cry. No one else took up the cry, but they all appeared to be satisfied enough.

"I'll do my best for you," Merriwether promised.

"We know you shall," J. Aubrey said grandly. "Our faith rests with you now, sir, quite as much as our gratitude already had."

EIGHTEEN

AH, HUMAN NATURE. It was one of those rare and agreeable things, a trait in which a gentleman could place his full faith and confidence.

Merriwether and his friend Capt. Zeebruge were cheerfully fleecing J. Aubrey Whitford and his Baja expeditioners. Or thought they were.

The poor fellows would simply have to learn that a wolf in sheep's clothing provides no fleece.

And J. Aubrey knew just who could teach them.

"It's sorry I am, gentlemen, but I have no choice in it," Zeebruge said in a lugubrious voice. "If I accept your party for passage, I must forego the deck cargo I'd counted on for this voyage. I owe it to my shareholders to bring them back a profit. I can't carry you all the way to the coast of Texas for less than eighty-five dollars per passenger. And at that, you see, I make nothing for myself. 'Tis only as an accommodation to Mr. Merriwether here and in consideration of your plight that I give you this price. Eighty and five per head, gentlemen. I can do you no better."

Bolliger and Smith turned to look at their expedition leader. J. Aubrey had insisted that a delegation of expeditioners accompany him at the passage negotiations; he'd wanted witnesses to the effort and the expense he would encounter on their behalf. The men had talked it over among themselves as recently as last night. No one had anticipated fees this large. Not with the kindly Mr. Merriwether interceding with the ship's captain on their behalf.

J. Aubrey looked pained. He dropped his eyes. He wrung his hands. He sat back in the uncomfortable chair and ran a finger

inside his collar as if to hint that it choked him. His appearance
was that of a man in acute discomfort.

In fact he was having some difficulty keeping from chuckling.

"Eighty-five dollars. That would be . . ."

"Two thousand five hundred and fifty," Zeebruge helpfully
provided the total.

"There are only twenty-nine expedition members. . . ."

"Plus yourself, sir. Unless you intend to remain in St. Augustine."

"No," J. Aubrey said quickly. "Certainly not. Desert men
whom I have come to think of as friends as well as clients?
Never. But eighty-five dollars?"

"It is the very best I can do. A normal passage fee all the way
to Texas would be a hundred twenty, hundred forty dollars, I
assure you. Ask anyone, if you wish."

"Oh, I don't question your veracity, sir. Not at all." In point
of fact, J. Aubrey had already asked. And Capt. Zeebruge was
quite correct. Normal passage would be in the hundred-and-
twenty-dollar range. On a vessel equipped for passenger accommodation and with full bill of fare provided. Half that for this
gentleman's offered deck space.

J. Aubrey's only uncertainty in the matter was the proportion
of profit allotted to Merriwether's pocket. Five dollars? Likely
more.

Ah, yes. Human nature. *So* dependable.

"We accept," J. Aubrey said reluctantly. Bolliger laid a com-
forting hand on J. Aubrey's forearm.

"Two thousand five hundred fifty dollars, sir. Cash, if you
please."

"Yes." J. Aubrey reached inside his coat. Brought out a sheaf
of bearer drafts and peeled off three of them.

"What d'you have there, sir?"

Wordlessly, J. Aubrey shoved the drafts across the table for
Zeebruge and Merriwether to inspect.

"These aren't cash."

"As good as," J. Aubrey explained. "My banker in New York

advised me to carry our funds in his drafts. There is his signature. On that line there, see? He told me it wouldn't be safe for us to travel with coin in unsettled country. Too much danger from highwaymen and brigands and such. He assured me these drafts would be acceptable anywhere."

Zeebruge frowned. And got a look of warning from Merriwether. "I can deposit them through my bank in Charleston," he said. "I'll credit your . . . the amount, that is . . . to your account here, Kurt. I don't see a problem with this."

Lovely, J. Aubrey thought. The worthy gentlemen really were reaping themselves a fine profit on this transaction. Otherwise Merriwether wouldn't be so quick to keep it from escaping their grasp. It was entirely possible, perhaps even probable, that the owners of Capt. Zeebruge's ship would never know about the passengers who would enjoy the accommodations of their vessel. Merriwether and Zeebruge might well be planning to split the entire passage fee between themselves, the shareholders never the wiser for it. That would make for a tidy profit indeed.

"If you say so," Zeebruge said.

"Of course, Kurt. First Continental? Excellent reputation. Entirely reliable."

"Never heard of them," Zeebruge complained.

"I certainly have," Merriwether told him. "First-rate bank."

And so they were, J. Aubrey agreed. Not that he'd ever had an account there, of course. But he might. Someday.

"If you could provide a pen and ink," J. Aubrey suggested, "I shall countersign the drafts. On that line there, I believe. Can't have your bank questioning them now, can we, ha ha. Everything on the up and up. Oh, and while you're getting the pen for my endorsement, Mr. Merriwether, would you mind bringing my change for the difference? I believe you will notice that the drafts are in thousand dollar increments. That leaves, um, something like four hundred fifty dollars in change owing, I believe." He smiled.

Merriwether smiled. Zeebruge smiled. Bolliger and Mr. Smith smiled.

J. Aubrey loved it when everyone was happy.

NINETEEN

THIS SEA VOYAGE was easier than the first had been, if only because the travelers were now more accustomed to shipboard life—and motion—than they had been. Even J. Aubrey was able to look at the waves now and then without wanting to run for the rail.

Capt. Zeebruge's *Mona Marie* loaded a scanty cargo of salt and salt beef at St. Augustine—this was the man who had to give up deck cargo so he would have room to take passengers aboard? it was to laugh, J. Aubrey thought happily—and carried them south around the tip end of the Floridas and back north again to a port called Cedar Key. Cedar Key was little bigger than an ant hill but was considerably busier. The *Mona Marie* exchanged beef and salt there for a full cargo of lumber, and then itself lumbered, riding low and heavy in the water, off into the green waters of the Gulf of Mexico.

"We'll be there soon won't we, Mr. Whitford?" the expeditioners asked repeatedly. Although by now every one of them knew at least as much about the geography of this area as J. Aubrey did.

"Soon."

He stood at the bowsprit with his chin held high and pointing toward Texas, and knew he cut a fine figure in the clothing he'd had tailored in St. Augustine. There had been, after all, the infusion of welcome cash into his pockets, and J. Aubrey was not a man to allow opportunity to slide past unsaluted.

"Just a few more weeks now and we'll be in the Baja?"

"Undoubtedly," J. Aubrey agreed. Well, maybe not *everyone* had thoroughly familiarized himself with the maps and charts.

This Baja was somewhere beneath California. Which was said to be quite a ways distant from Texas.

On the other hand, how much could there be in between? Very little, apparently. J. Aubrey's concern at the moment was that Baja be far enough away from Texas for him to have time enough en route to generate income-earning opportunity for himself.

If the two really were only a few weeks apart . . . He would worry about that when the time came.

For the nonce, he was content to stand at the railing with a far-gazing look in his eye, and with the full faith and confidence of his expeditioners solidly behind him.

And all the while the faithful Capt. Zeebruge and his *Mona Marie* ploughed onward toward some place called Port Lavaca.

TWENTY

J. AUBREY stood at the deck railing and frowned.

He'd thought St. Augustine was bad with its heat and humidity and bugs?

Port Lavaca was everything St. Augustine had been. And less.

What Port Lavaca lacked, mostly, was trees. J. Aubrey had never seen a place before that had no trees. Not unless you wanted to count New York, which made up for the lack by substituting buildings and lamp posts and the like.

Here there was . . . darn little, that was what there was here.

Sea water and sea grass and sun-baked sand. A few ramshackle sun-baked hovels. A rickety, sun-baked wharf.

No trees, no hills, no hint of shade anywhere in sight.

J. Aubrey wondered what he'd done to deserve being here.

"Look at it, gentlemen. Just look," he said, turning to his expeditioners with a broad and genial smile. "The land of opportunity one small step removed." He made a wide, sweeping gesture that encompassed the whole of the dreary, sun-baked horizon.

Bolliger made a face that looked as sour as J. Aubrey felt. Most of the others looked skeptical at best. Only Smith and his pair of cronies seemed indifferent to the sight before them.

"Watch that line, watch that line now. Don't let it kink." The *Mona Marie* was being warped slowly in against the meager hint of breeze that existed here. Oarsmen in small boats had dragged the vessel close enough to reach with cables from ashore, and now she was being hauled the last few yards to her docking.

J. Aubrey sniffed. He was no seaman, not hardly, but even he could see how poor a port this one was. There were no booms or tackle here to speak of. The cargo would have to be laboriously removed by hand. Probably that would mean it would be late before his expedition members got their equipment off. Still, that should give him time to survey the situation locally, and see what might best be turned to advantage here.

He spent a moment passing encouraging words among his expeditioners, then made his way back—aft, it was called—to see Capt. Zeebruge. That worthy gentleman, fortunately, would not discover he'd been flimflammed until he returned to St. Augustine, at the very earliest.

"Careful, Mr. Whitford. Mind you don't trip on the bollard there. Hate to lose you overboard at this late stage, ha ha."

J. Aubrey dutifully smiled. Capt. Zeebruge had been most cordial the whole trip long. But then Zeebruge thought he was taking poor and trusting Mr. Whitford, didn't he?

"What can I do for you, sir?" Zeebruge asked.

"I was hoping to prevail on your kindness one more time before we reluctantly part company, sir," J. Aubrey said.

"Anything I can do, Mr. Whitford. Anything at all."

"I was hoping, sir, you could grant me introductions to the, um, gentlemen of quality hereabouts. And perhaps a letter of introduction as well?"

"Of course, Mr. Whitford. Glad to do it. I believe you will find me not unknown in Port Lavaca and inland as far as Victoria also. Glad to help you any way I can."

"Thank you, captain. You have been most gracious and accommodating on our voyage. We are in your debt, sir." Which was somewhat truer than the good captain knew.

"No problem, Mr. Whitford. I'll be able to go below quick as we're tied fast here. I'll jot that letter down for you, then you can accompany me ashore and you can meet the gentry of Port Lavaca. No problem with that, sir."

J. Aubrey smiled and bowed and waited, in somewhat better spirits now, for the docking process to be completed.

TWENTY-ONE

CAPT. ZEEBRUGE actually was known and respected in Port Lavaca. And as good as his word when it came to making some judicious introductions. The leading citizens of the tiny port community gave the expeditioners a hearty welcome.

J. Aubrey suspected that Zeebruge had primed the pump for him (bless that man's heart; why, J. Aubrey hadn't even had to find a way to make the suggestion to him). He had informed these backwoods Texans—well, if there'd been any woods to be back in, that is—that the expedition was in trouble and had money to buy their way out. There was nothing like the endorsement of a trusted friend to smooth the path.

Not that he could reasonably expect to convert all his carefully fabricated bank draft documents into cash here. Probably there was not nine thousand dollars of hard money to be found in all of Port Lavaca, J. Aubrey suspected . . . or in all of Texas, judging from what little of it they'd seen so far.

Still, something was always better than nothing.

What J. Aubrey needed was money, naturally. Here, or very soon afterward with the helpful assistance of these bucolic folk, he should be able to pass his drafts. Even at a discount if necessary. Then, why, it should be the simplest matter possible for him to slip away from the expedition group and . . .

He would work that out when the time came.

Although what a gentleman was expected to do with himself in such uncivilized surroundings—except, of course, to make his way swiftly elsewhere—well, all that was beyond J. Aubrey's considerable comprehension.

He practically shuddered whenever he looked about him in this uncertain country.

Dreary, that was what it was. Practically foreign, no matter that it had been rescued from independence and taken on as a part of the union. A most unwise decision, in J. Aubrey's opinion.

The countryside itself was dreary, and its few citizens were worse, if that was possible. Bumpkins of ragged clothing and unkempt appearance. J. Aubrey had neither understanding nor sympathy for any man without pride enough to keep his person tidy.

He sniffed, dismissing the Texans, and pondered just where in this miserable place a man might hope to find a banker or a broker suitable to his needs.

"There's no place t' be puttin' you folks up here," the town mayor drawled, albeit with no hint of apology in his tone. The man—mayor he styled himself, incredible!—wore no collar and was in shirt-sleeves. *Shirt-sleeves,* if anyone could believe that, which J. Aubrey couldn't. Not even the poorest coat but in shirt-sleeves. And this was the town's leading citizen?

"I got me some wagons an' mules," the mayor droned on in a nasal mush-mouth. "I'll carry you folks over t' Victoria."

J. Aubrey gave the poor fellow a gracious smile. "We are in your debt, sir."

His choice of wording was deliberate. Perhaps this bumpkin was better founded than he appeared. None of the normal rules of judgment seemed to apply here, certainly. J. Aubrey was quite willing to open the door to a discussion of transportation fees with the mayor of Port Lavaca. There might yet be opportunity to convert paper into coin here.

"Naw, you'd do as much fer me, I reckon." The mayor gave J. Aubrey an aw-shucks grin and turned away.

J. Aubrey blinked.

TWENTY-TWO

GOOD LORD, this couldn't be happening. Or, um, could it? He pondered. Realized that it couldn't and tried to prepare himself for whatever was about to come.

The wagons deposited J. Aubrey Whitford and his merry band of Baja-bound expeditioners at a livery barn at the inland community of Victoria, where there was room enough for them to store their possessions and spread their blankets on straw.

Two wagons. Rather large wagons, at that. Two drivers. Three Mexican helpers. Sixteen mules employed. Miles of travel and hours of labor involved.

Why, the men sent with the wagons even went so far as to help the expeditioners unload everything into the barn.

And now they were smiling, shaking hands, issuing hopes of good fortune, waving . . . and they hadn't yet said a single word about payment for all this service provided by the hayseed mayor of Port Lavaca.

What was the man up to?

J. Aubrey was becoming suspicious. And more than a little nervous.

That man had to be up to *some*thing.

Something especially devious, J. Aubrey judged.

But where was the scam? Where the sting? Just what *was* it he was preparing to smite them with?

No one would go to all this trouble for total strangers and expect nothing in return for it.

Could it have something to do with the man remaining back at Port Lavaca? He'd pleaded pressing business. Humph. What business in Port Lavaca could possibly have been pressing?

Surely he didn't hope to convince anyone that the Baja expedition stole these services from him and then refused to pay. It would have been easier by far to simply charge an outrageous fee to begin with. J. Aubrey would have understood that. In fact, he quite expected it.

Yet so far no mention of payment had been made.

This was becoming worrisome.

The Mexican laborers grinned and bobbed their heads and said something to the expeditioners.

The Texans who had driven the wagons said their goodbyes and smiled.

The Mexicans turned and all trooped to the nearer wagon. They climbed into the back of the tall, towering freight wagon and sank out of sight behind the sideboards.

One of the Texans crawled up onto the driving box of his rig. The other came sauntering over toward J. Aubrey with a curiously loose and slouching gait. The slouch, J. Aubrey had already concluded, was the preferred national posture of Texas.

J. Aubrey smiled. At last. The period of waiting and worry would be ending now. Whatever it was that man in Port Lavaca planned, surely it would be executed now. Surely now he would show his hand. In particular he would show how he intended to place that hand deep into J. Aubrey Whitford's tailored pocket. This grinning, slouching wagon driver obviously had his instructions. Ha! This was J. Aubrey's meat. He was capable of being quite as slippery as the best of them. And was head and shoulders above the common lot.

"Hope you fellas do good out there, heah?" the wagon driver said. "T'was a pleasure meetin' up with you folks." He chuckled and extended his hand.

J. Aubrey shook it. There was no harm in that. He arranged a genial smile on his handsome features and spoke the requisite pleasantries and waited for the Texan to show his scheme.

"Y'all take care now, heah? 'Bye."

The wagon driver turned away and slouched on to his rig. He climbed onto the box, picked up his driving lines and shook the sleepy mules into motion, wheeling the wagon back in the direction from which they'd just come.

He left J. Aubrey standing incredulous in the twilight outside a livery barn on the outskirts of Victoria, Texas.

TWENTY-THREE

"MR. WHITFORD, I presume."

J. Aubrey smiled and was quick to remove his freshly brushed silk hat before he shook hands with the gentleman and bowed to the lady.

"Alvin Tattersal at your service, sir, and my wife Leona."

"My pleasure, sir, ma'am."

Tattersal at least wore a suit. Not a good one perhaps but a suit nonetheless. He was half a head shorter than J. Aubrey and half as large again around the girth. A man of some substance here, no doubt.

His wife was . . . toothsome. Plump. Younger by some years than her mate. Buxom and broad of hip. J. Aubrey found her to be delightfully attractive. He gave her the benefit of one of his finest smiles and bent over her dimpled hand, startling her into a blush and a simper. Tattersal looked on quite happily.

"I understand your party has had certain difficulties, Mr. Whitford," Tattersal said.

"Difficulties," J. Aubrey repeated, mouthing the word as if tasting it. "Yes, sir, I believe one could reasonably lay a claim to there having been difficulties." He felt considerably better now, actually. He believed he was beginning to understand. That devious chap from Port Lavaca had brought them here not out of the goodness of his heart but to set the travelers up. It wasn't he who planned to extract a fleece from these sheep, but his partner Tattersal. J. Aubrey definitely felt better now, if only because a man can always face what lies before him; it is the unknown that is worrisome.

"We want you to know, Mr. Whitford, that we will do whatever we can to make you all feel welcome here. Feel free to use the old barn like it was your own. And of course we will help find you transportation west. In the meantime, sir, you must all consider yourselves guests of our fair community."

"Kind of you, Mr. Tattersal. Most kind." J. Aubrey beamed and rocked heel-and-toe. Tattersal smiled. Leona Tattersal smiled.

"Well, I see your people have your supper about ready, Mr. Whitford. We wouldn't want to keep you from it. Sorry we didn't have any advance notice you were coming or we could've laid on a barbecue for you folks. We'll do that tomorrow, eh?" He chuckled. J. Aubrey wondered what a barbecue was.

The man shook J. Aubrey's hand again. Mrs. Tattersal smiled again.

Then the two of them turned and just . . . walked away.

No mention of fees for the transportation, nor of payment for the privilege of occupying a barn.

J. Aubrey began to worry again.

TWENTY-FOUR

IF HE HADN'T BEEN so concerned about when the second shoe would drop, J. Aubrey would have been quite thoroughly enjoying himself.

A barbecue, it seemed, was the Texas equivalent of a gala, although with a rustic theme about it.

The people had begun to gather in the forenoon and were still coming.

First there had been a handful of men who dug a firepit and erected a pair of iron tripods, then a wagon came bearing an entire beef—inconceivable but true, an entire beef—on a massive spit.

A second and larger firepit was dug and a roaring fire started, using an iron-hard and thorny sort of wood locally harvested. As soon as coals were to be had they were transferred to the shallow pit beneath the spit. Men and boys took turns rotating the roasting beef, while others kept the fire blazing to create still more coals. The meat had been cooking inside its own juices for the better part of the day now. J. Aubrey had never seen such a thing, nor had any of his expeditioners.

The food preparations might be the focus of the affair but were hardly all of it. While the hundreds of pounds of meat sizzled, people streamed in by foot and wagon and horseback. There were scores of them gathered now. They brought baskets and hampers with them. More foods to snack on while the main course cooked. And they brought musical instruments. Violins —they called them "fiddles"—and fifes. Cymbals and cornets. Homemade things fashioned from gourds and washtubs. There were even two handsomely constructed accordions manned by Germans with bristling mustaches and bulging bellies.

A dance floor of sorts had been created by the simple expedient of beating a patch of earth bare with the stomping of many feet.

Plank and sawhorse trestle tables sprang out of the ground like so many mushrooms, and were quickly covered with quilts and foodstuffs.

A hat was passed and kegs of beer produced. Off on the fringes there were jugs of somewhat more potent substance passing from hand to hand.

The members of the Whitford Expedition to the Newest Baja Discoveries were the center of attention.

Junius Hankins had been dancing much of the afternoon with a woman who was at least twice his age, and probably twice his energy as well. Hankins was flushed and sweating and close to collapse but the old lady wouldn't allow him off the dance floor.

Harry Field sat spraddle-legged on the ground wearing a silly expression and a straw sombrero. He had been imbibing, but no one seemed to mind. Daniel Warren stood arm in arm with several lanky Texans who were teaching him the words to risqué songs quite loudly sung. All the ladies, fortunately, affected not to notice. Even Smith and his cronies had unbent so far as to lose their frowns.

J. Aubrey helped himself to a cup of tart, slightly greenish punch—he had no idea what was in the stuff but enjoyed it—and a leg of crisply fried chicken that someone had brought to ward off the ravages of hunger while the beef roasted.

If only he understood what all of this was supposed to cost him he really could have enjoyed himself.

TWENTY-FIVE

J. AUBREY'S HEAD POUNDED. His tongue felt thick and lumpy, and there was a taste of bile lurking in the back of his throat. This morning wasn't nearly so much fun as last night had been.

He sat up, cleared his throat loudly and dressed. The rest of his expeditioners were scattered about snoring on the floor of the barn. J. Aubrey frowned and quickly checked his coat pockets.

With a groan of relief he realized that all his things were still there. The bank drafts. The cash he had remaining after the bit of good fortune in St. Augustine. Most importantly his pen case was intact. It was a good thing, though, that he wasn't required to fabricate any more documents today. If his hands were as shaky as the rest of him seemed to be at this moment, that would have been an exercise in complete futility.

When he set the weight of his fine hat onto his head he winced.

He stumbled outside, found the necessary facility and made a face when once more he surveyed the scene of last night's merriment.

It looked more the aftermath of a battle than a dance.

The planks and sawhorses that so recently had been trestle tables now were just so much flotsam on a sea of filth. Containers lay here. Bones there. Rags, paper, shattered gourds, even a few oddments of clothing lay scattered about.

Dogs snarled over the division of spoils when it came to the disposition of what little remained of the beef carcass, while birds waited nearby to cluster to whatever the dogs might leave behind.

J. Aubrey upended an unsplit section of firelog and sat on it with his massive head cradled tenderly in his hands.

He groaned and snuffled and gave serious thought to seeking out a cave he might crawl into. Hibernation seemed an attractive plan at the moment. Say for the next three or four months. By then he might feel better. A little.

"Good morning, Mr. Whitford."

J. Aubrey winced. He looked up to see Mr. Tattersal standing there with another, smaller man.

The last J. Aubrey had seen of Tattersal, the fellow was roaring in song and dragging his wife off toward the shadows. This morning he was freshly shaved and almost dapper. He seemed absolutely none the worse for wear.

The man with Tattersal had also been present yesterday. J. Aubrey could not remember his name, but seemed to recall seeing him engaged in an impromptu display of fisticuffs with two considerably larger men. The memory was reinforced by the fact that now the man's face was purpled with bruises, and there were freshly crusted scabs forming where his mouth and the side of his nose had been split. He had taken quite a pummeling.

There was something else about the incident that . . .

J. Aubrey winced again. Of course. The two men this fellow'd been fighting with were Smith's two chums. What were their names? It hurt his head to think this morning. Brown and Black. Of course. How original of them. J. Aubrey sighed and stood up to greet the locals.

"Good morning, gentlemen." He felt slightly dizzy and was unsteady on his feet. Tattersal and friend must have seen—they couldn't possibly have missed it—for they both chuckled sympathetically.

"Care for a hair o' the dog?" the small man asked, reaching for the hip pocket of his bib overalls.

"No. Please." J. Aubrey looked away so fast that his head became light and swimmy, and he nearly lost his balance. He could hear the locals laughing but, dammit, the mere thought of taking a drink now was revolting.

The little man put his flask away, and J. Aubrey tried to gain control of himself. A man needs his wits about him if he wants to meet trouble and turn it aside.

Surely these two had come here seeking redress for that fight and the battering the little man had taken.

The question, really, was whether they would be satisfied with an apology. Or if their true aim was retributive compensation. Compensation, likely. That seemed the only rational explanation. Otherwise why their cheerful eagerness at a time like this? J. Aubrey felt like he wanted to be sick.

Surely the members of the expedition would not expect him to provide bail money for errant expeditioners. Surely that should come out of Brown's and Black's own pockets.

And if the men were locked up—J. Aubrey hadn't noticed a jail in Victoria but there would have to be one—would the expeditioners demand to linger here until Brown and Black were freed? What would be the effect on the others if their leader wanted to press on and was thwarted? What the effect if he recommended in the reverse of that question?

J. Aubrey felt quite incapable of coping with these questions at the moment.

"Sure was a fun barbecue, weren't it, Mr. Whitford?" the small man asked, his voice and demeanor pleasant.

"Oh my, yes," J. Aubrey said dryly. Tattersal chuckled again. "You, uh," J. Aubrey began, stopped, tried again. "I am sure, sir, that we were introduced last night. But my memory seems a trifle sluggish this morning. Would you mind . . ."

The little fellow laughed. Loudly. Rather painfully loud, in fact. J. Aubrey gulped and tried to ward off a wave of nausea.

"Hay, Mr. Whitford. Quentin Hay?"

J. Aubrey had no recall of that name whatsoever.

"You c'n call me Squint. You know?"

J. Aubrey gave him a blank look.

"Quentin shorts down t' Quent an' becomes Quint an' that leads to Squint. See?"

"I see. Yes." Sort of. Not that he particularly cared. At this moment J. Aubrey was regretting the impulse to rise. He wished he could crawl back to whatever bed he'd made for himself last night—or had been dumped onto, whichever—and start this day all over again. Tomorrow perhaps.

"You don't remember a bit of it, do you?" Tattersal asked in a voice that was not unkind.

"I do not," J. Aubrey confessed. Which seemed for some reason to amuse both these Texans.

"You stay out here long enough, Whitford, we'll learn you t' hold your likker proper."

"Thank you, I'm sure."

Squint Hay giggled. The sound of it was quite startling, coming from so evil-looking a little man.

And he was, bruises and batterings aside, a sly and shifty-looking sort. Small and dark and wiry, with unkempt clothing and few teeth visible when he laughed. His hair was greasy and his face pinched and weasely. Yet Tattersal acted toward Hay as if the two were equals, and Tattersal was a man of substance here.

It occurred to J. Aubrey that one of the striking things he'd noticed during the gala—barbecue—before he became incapable of paying attention to such things, that is—was that everyone here acted like they were all on equal footing. Even men of such obviously disparate habit and background as Tattersal and Hay.

"What Alvin is tryin' t' remind you of, Whitford, is that I'm the one gonna take you an' your party west outa here," Hay said once he was done giggling.

"You are?"

Squint Hay hooted and dug an elbow into Tattersal's ribs. Tattersal's response was, oddly, amusement rather than resentment at the familiarity.

"I told you he wouldn't remember nothing, Alvin."

"So you did, Squint, so you did."

"C'mon, Whitford. We'll have us some breakfast an' get some business done while we're about it."

J. Aubrey did *not* feel up to this. Not that he was being given much choice about it. The two locals flanked him, took him by the arms and squired him off toward the main business district of dumpy little Victoria, before J. Aubrey had wit enough collected to question or to protest.

It occurred to J. Aubrey as they walked that this Squint Hay person hadn't yet gotten around to mentioning the beating Brown and Black had given him. But then most probably he would be considering that when he negotiated the travel arrangements for the group as a whole.

J. Aubrey concentrated what little energy he had into readying himself for this contest of wills that was being forced upon him.

TWENTY-SIX

ALL RIGHT, so where was the clinker? J. Aubrey couldn't so much as enjoy his meal—which he had no idea who was paying for; no check had been presented and no mention made about cost—for wondering when the shoe was going to fall.

"Now y'see, Aubrey," Hay was nattering, tiny bits of crumb-cake dislodging from his mustache as he spoke, "I happen t' have this sister out in 'del Norte. El Paso del Norte, that is. Haven't seen Esther in I dunno how long, an' I been thinking about her. So it wouldn't hurt me none t' haul you an' your people that far. I mean, I got the wagons anyway. Freighting, that's what I do. So Alvin here comes up with the idea that I carry you folks out there, an' it goes down pretty easy with me when he says it. So if you want me to, well, I reckon we can strike us a deal."

At last. J. Aubrey felt relieved. Greatly relieved, in fact. He maintained his composure. His smile never faltered. "And what deal was it that you had in mind, Mr. Hay?"

Hay grinned. "Squint. Thought we'd worked it out a'ready that I'm Squint an' you're Aubrey. We ain't much for talking at things th' long way around 'em."

"I stand corrected, Squint."

"As fer the deal, Aubrey . . ." Squint Hay peered off toward the ceiling with his eyes unfocused and dreamy. J. Aubrey could just *imagine* the thoughts this evil-looking little man must be having. How much he had to pay back to Tattersal. Who of course still would have to cover his split with the fellow in Port Lavaca. Then how much Hay would want for himself, of course. The question really came down to how much these two would think they could extract from the Whitford Expedition.

J. Aubrey's smile turned a trifle sly. They might find they

could take him for much more than they anticipated, actually. Provided, that is, the amount could be floated via the local bank or money lender, and paid by way of a draft against the First Continental.

If he could hold the transportation charges in the vicinity of five hundred, J. Aubrey would be satisfied. Anything under six hundred would still allow him to pocket a reasonable return, in fact.

Call it five hundred, then, and a bargain for the movement of more than a score of men and all their personal possessions and gold-mining equipage.

The "change" from his bank draft would weigh nicely in his purse, along with the amount already gained in Florida. J. Aubrey calculated that he might yet come out of this with several thousand cash in hand. At that point he could quietly decamp without having to feel that this expedition idea was ending in failure.

"Let's say, oh, let's say fifty," Squint Hay finally declared.

"Pardon me?" J. Aubrey blurted.

"Fifty dollars, Aubrey. I reckon that'd be fair. Give me a little likker money when I get to 'del Norte an' keep my mules in fodder while I visit with Esther. I don't see as I could do it for much less'n that, though. Sorry to tell it to you, but I think I got t' get fifty dollars outa this trip."

"And this El Paso del Norte place is . . . ?" J. Aubrey pointed rather vaguely toward the west.

"What would you say, Alvin? Four weeks west o' here. Five if the water ain't good out there."

"About that I should think," Tattersal agreed. "Depending on water and the Comanches, of course."

"Comanches?" J. Aubrey repeated. It was a word he thought he might have heard somewhere before, although in precisely what connection he could no longer recall.

"Injuns, Aubrey. Wild Injuns. Sons o' bitches."

"But don't worry," Tattersal said. "They stay mostly to themselves far to the north of where you will be."

"Be honest with the man, Alvin," Hay chided.

Tattersal shrugged.

"The thing is, Aubrey," Hay said, leaning forward now and propping his elbows on the table, "a few years back a bunch o' Comanches left off their usual raiding routes down inta Mexico an' come by Victoria here. Treed the whole damn town they did. Run off everybody they didn't kill an' looted ever' damn building an' shed you see out there."

"But those days are over," Tattersal insisted. "We have Colt's repeating firearms now. They would get a far different reception if they tried that again today."

It occurred to J. Aubrey, however, that events happening in Victoria were not what he had to be concerned about. The Whitford Expedition was not intending to remain in Victoria, after all.

In the midst of J. Aubrey's sudden concerns with the possibility of actual wild Indian raiders, the matter of Squint Hay's fee became submerged. And left dangling at the absurdly low price of fifty dollars.

That figure was not—he realized some hours later—sufficiently high to justify the cashing of a bank draft here. Drat it.

He consoled himself with the knowledge that he'd really had little choice in the matter anyway.

After all, how does a gentleman go about negotiating a fee ten times *higher* than the amount proposed to him.

J. Aubrey would simply have to pay Hay's fee out of pocket, and look for another opportunity to convert his bank drafts to cash. And the sooner the better. Very much more of this traveling nonsense and they might actually reach the Baja. A disquieting thought indeed, that one.

He hid his inward shudderings and misgivings as he conveyed the "good" news to his bleary-eyed expeditioners.

TWENTY-SEVEN

THE EXPEDITIONERS were excited, even if a trifle subdued by the lingering aftereffects from the night before. J. Aubrey accepted their cheers with becoming modesty.

He noted that Smith and Brown and Black were absent from the collection at the moment. But no matter. If they failed to appear at all they were certainly entitled to leave the expedition when and how they chose.

As for the others, they seemed eager now to press on to the promised gold fields of the Baja.

"Our good friend Mr. Hay asks me to inform you, gentlemen, that he is preparing his wagons for travel. Preparing them even as we speak. He will deliver them to us this evening for the purposes of loading our possessions. The Whitford Expedition will depart Victoria promptly at dawn on the morrow."

"How far is it to the Baja now?" someone in the crowd asked.

"We remain more than a month away from our goal," J. Aubrey told him with some degree of certainty. That seemed only reasonable since Hay had said this El Paso del Norte place was that far away.

Or was it possible that El Paso del Norte was actually in the Baja? J. Aubrey considered, somewhat too late for it to matter, that he really should have asked. He had, after all, only an imprecise idea of where the Baja was. And no concept whatsoever of where El Paso del Norte was to be found in relation to it.

"Tomorrow, gentlemen," he said. "Tomorrow at the dawning we are off on our venture once again."

TWENTY-EIGHT

SQUINT HAY'S CAVALCADE was quite a procession. Certainly more than anything J. Aubrey might have anticipated. The little man brought four mule-drawn wagons to haul a load that had required only two wagons to get them from Port Lavaca to Victoria. Hay insisted that none of the wagons be too heavily burdened and supervised the loading process himself so that the weights were evenly balanced on the running gear.

In addition to the freight wagons, though, there were also three light mud wagons to carry the expedition members comfortably aboard, two smallish springboard wagons containing foodstuffs and other unidentifiable supplies, and a ramshackle and obviously homemade device to serve as a kitchen on wheels. And eight, by actual count, mule-drawn *carretas* with single axles mounted in huge, man-tall wooden wheels. These last were loaded to overflowing with dark-haired women and, mostly, big-eyed children, not a one of whom seemed to speak a word of English.

Apparently this trip of necessity for the Whitford Expedition came at a convenient time for a westward emigration of half the Mexican population of southern Texas. Or so J. Aubrey assumed. Apart from that he could conceive of no clear explanation for this sudden departure of so many.

Many? J. Aubrey had seen towns with less population than the number of people now intending to depart Victoria for El Paso del Norte in the west. Seen such towns? J. Aubrey had grown up in a town considerably smaller. This was like placing that village —not that he particularly wanted to think back to it—on wheels and dragging it away.

He couldn't understand a word the Mexicans were saying, of course, but he could certainly attest that there were a great many words being spoken.

Mexican drivers on the large wagons shouted back and forth among themselves and the women and children on the carts. They called goodbyes—presumably—to a throng of waving well-wishers who had assembled to see the procession off, and alternated between giving grins and scowls to their counterparts on the other rigs. The whole affair was quite as noisy as it was confusing.

If J. Aubrey found himself nonplused by this unexpected collection of mules, vehicles and humanity, he was completely flabbergasted by what appeared to be an overnight transformation in Captain—as he now asserted he might reasonably be called— Quentin Hay.

Yesterday Hay had been a typical Texan. Which is to say loose, slovenly, slouching, tobacco chewing, unkempt, slow speaking, slower moving . . . in sum, on the downward end of any scale of respectability.

This morning Squint Hay was . . . vibrant. Quick, energetic, sure in his movements. Even his appearance seemed to have transformed somehow, although his clothing was unchanged from what he had been wearing yesterday.

The great difference, of course, was that today Capt. Hay was mounted on horseback. And on the back of a horse, Squint Hay seemed an utterly different human being from the lackadaisical fellow J. Aubrey thought he'd already met.

Rather than sitting atop the horse and saddle, Hay seemed to attach himself to the animal, as if he were a natural growth rising out of the center of this new creation that melded horse and man into one beast. His movements aboard the big saddle seemed as natural as breathing, and his control over the horse was positively mystifying.

J. Aubrey had seen gentlemen ride, naturally, although it was not an activity he himself had ever chanced to engage in. And from time to time he had paid somewhat greater attention to ladies dressed in closely fitted riding habits while they jogged and jostled atop a handsome horse. It was his experience that a gentleman, such as himself, could learn a great deal by observing a lady and her mount. The more delicate members of the fairer sex tend to perch uncertainly atop a steed and follow docilely amid the pack. Herd. Whatever. Those were the ladies J. Aubrey liked to cultivate. He had learned to avoid ladies who chose to ride spirited mounts that required domination, for those women commonly wished to dominate male humans quite as much as they did male equines.

His observations had also taught him that riding a horse is a matter to be approached with skill but also with trepidation. It requires complete concentration on the task at hand. And both hands are definitely needed in order to maintain control over half a ton of stupid, flighty beast.

At least that was far and away the impression he had gained after some years of close and considered observation.

None of the gentlemen and ladies J. Aubrey ever observed before this morning received their instruction in the equestrian arts from Squint Hay.

Hay seemed to pay attention to anything *but* his horse.

He talked, he pointed, he gave instructions in two languages. He waved, slouched, spat, scratched.

Not once did he appear to pay the slightest attention to the horse that moved underneath him with all the closeness of connection as an overlarge carbuncle growing out of Hay's own backside.

Controlling straps—reins, J. Aubrey thought they were called —were supposed to be tended with diligence and care and certainly with both fists firmly applied. Or so it had seemed until now.

Squint Hay barely bothered with them. Oh, he kept casual hold of them with one hand, true. But the appearance given was that he was more keeping the leather straps from falling to the ground than using them to control anything. After all, they dangled limp and loose against the horse's neck, and neither Hay nor the animal seemed to pay them much mind.

Yet somehow—J. Aubrey could not fathom it in the slightest —the horse seemed to move exactly as Hay desired. It could spin, stop, leap about, even shuffle sideways to his whim. Yet Squint never once bothered to speak to the animal or look at it or openly direct it in any way that J. Aubrey could see.

And the captain of the wagon train certainly kept the beast moving. Dashing from one end of the column to the other. Column? There hadn't been a column to begin with. Only a confused assortment of many vehicles, animals and people being assembled into a loud, dusty mass.

Now there was a column.

Squint shouted in Spanish and got laughter and more Spanish back in return. Whips cracked. Dogs barked. And all of a sudden there was a column. Passenger wagons to the fore. Freight wagons next. Light rigs next in line. And the *carretas* bringing up the rear.

J. Aubrey grabbed a roof bow to steady himself and held onto his top hat when his own mud wagon lurched forward to the head of the procession.

Off to the right he could see now that even this was not all of the train. Over there he could see more mounted men, men wearing huge hats and even bigger mustaches who were driving a herd of animals. Two herds actually, he soon realized. One of loose horses and mules, the other of cattle. Not work cattle either. These were no heavy-bodied oxen intended to draw the wagons if the mules should falter, but tall, skinny, long-legged bovines such as J. Aubrey had never seen before.

The column rolled slowly away from Victoria amid shouts and waving, and the herds of loose livestock were driven in behind.

By the time they were finally on the road, J. Aubrey judged the column was spread out in a thin line that was nearly a mile from front to rear. Incredible.

Dust from so many hoofs and wheels swirled into the still, summer air, and rose like a pale beacon to mark their passage across the face of this huge, dreary, empty land.

"I'll be damned," Junius Hankins mumbled from the seat adjacent to J. Aubrey's on the unpadded bench.

"Um, actually, so will I," J. Aubrey returned.

TWENTY-NINE

J. AUBREY STARED with some bewilderment at the place where they were supposed to sleep tonight.

"No need to worry about room at the inn here, eh?" Bolliger said. The man sounded actually cheerful.

J. Aubrey shuddered. "Hardly," he said.

Bolliger laughed and went off toward the wagon from where the expeditioners' personal possessions were being carried. He really didn't seem to mind. But . . .

It wasn't that J. Aubrey Whitford was overproud. He hadn't complained, not once, about sleeping in a barn at Victoria, in a warehouse before that; not a word in the meanest of circumstances aboard either ship.

But this . . .

Oh dear.

It was just . . . dirt. Not a building anywhere in *sight*.

It was *worse* than simple dirt. This dirt had spiny little cactuses growing in it. And rocks. Probably snakes too, for all J. Aubrey knew.

Why, there wasn't a decent and respectable tree or bush to be seen. The closest thing to it was more cactus, the only difference being that these other cactuses were bigger. Even the things J. Aubrey thought looked like trees were really cactuses. They must be. They were thorny enough that they almost had to be. Mesquite, Squint Hay said they were. As if that explained everything.

Texas. It was perfectly impossible. A loathsome and despicable place, to be sure.

If it weren't for the charm and allure of the money to be had by continuing this madness, J. Aubrey would sneak away this very night.

He sighed. Except of course he could not sneak away. Not from here. Not even if he had all the gold coin he could carry. Why, there was no telling what could happen to a person alone at night in an uncivilized place like this.

No, when he did say his silent goodbyes to the gentlemen of the Whitford Expedition, it would be in a city, by gum. And the bigger that city the better.

San Antonio would be the next city they would reach, Hay had said today. Another four days, he'd said.

J. Aubrey grimaced. Another four days. They'd made sixteen miles today. Or so Capt. Hay claimed. J. Aubrey certainly was not going to dispute the figure. Hay had been apologetic about the limited mileage. He said the pace would pick up once the loose stock became accustomed to the travel. J. Aubrey quite frankly didn't care a fig about the mileages. What he wanted was to reach this San Antonio place just as quickly as possible. There perhaps he could convert a draft or two and start merrily on his way.

"Good evening, Mr. Smith."

"Good evening, Mr. Whitford," the gold-seeker who called himself Smith returned.

"I haven't seen you for quite a while, Mr. Smith. Several days, I believe. I was beginning to fear that you and your friends missed the departure."

"Damn near did miss it," Smith admitted. "Mr. Brown and Mr. Black had a hard time getting themselves put back together after that pounding they took the other night."

"Pounding, Mr. Smith?"

"You must not a' seen it. They tangled with Mr. Hay at the barbecue. It was awful what that man did to them, Mr. Whitford. I thought for sure they were hurt permanent."

"No. That little man . . . ?"

"Aye," Smith confirmed. "But I wouldn't 've believed it either if I hadn't seen it myself." Smith clucked his tongue and shook his head. "Remind me never to cross that man, Mr. Whitford. And don't you think of it neither. Not that you would, of course," Smith hastily added.

"No, uh, of course not."

"You'd best get your blankets, Mr. Whitford, before they drive the wagon away. Unless you don't mind stumbling around in this mess. Personally I'm getting a little tired of thorns and stickers already." Smith's attitude seemed quite different from what it normally was. As if he intended to go out of his way now to make himself helpful and pleasant.

"Thank you for the advice, Mr. Smith. I'll see to my things immediately."

"Mind you stay away from the anthills too, Mr. Whitford. They're thick all through here."

"Thank you." J. Aubrey groaned. No doubt Texas ants bit. And whatever else might be encountered here. If the plants did, why should the bugs and the night creatures be any different?

He was looking forward to reaching San Antonio more and more.

THIRTY

J. AUBREY'S HOPES were high. High? They were soaring.

Today they would reach San Antonio. With any degree of luck, he could be done with his business and free of all this horror by tomorrow nightfall at the latest.

Ever since they left Victoria he'd been cultivating Squint Hay. Tonight they should be able to sleep in a proper hotel. Enjoy the inestimable luxury of a bath. With hot water no less. And then tomorrow, J. Aubrey could prevail upon Capt. Hay to make a few introductions. To the leading citizens of San Antonio. To, say, the banker here.

J. Aubrey smiled. He leaned down, jostling Avery Pollack's elbow as he did so, to slide a finger under the edge of his spat and vigorously scratch a welt on his ankle. He'd been right about the creatures here. The ants and everything else as well. Whatever didn't bite would sting. His ankles and a band around his waist were red and tender from a multitude of bites, and some foul little thing had raised a lump beneath his jaw. J. Aubrey hoped that bite didn't show so badly. He wanted to appear to best advantage when he met the bankers.

Still, thinking about that prospect, even the miseries of the bug bites could not keep the smile off his fine features today.

In San Antonio he could treat himself to some new linen. He would be able to afford it, after all. And if there were a decent tailor in town, some new shirts as well.

"Not far now, Aubrey," Hay said, reining his horse close to the mud wagon at the head of the long column. He pointed down the road to a break in the low trees.

That was another thing that added to J. Aubrey's high humor. The dreary and nearly barren coastal flats had been left behind, and now they were traveling amid real trees, oak and pecan and varieties J. Aubrey hadn't ever seen before, and real, green shrubs and succulent plants. The soil was less sandy here, much of it slightly red in color.

The wagons were approaching a small river now, J. Aubrey could see.

"Another couple miles, Aubrey. Be there early enough you can have you a bath afore supper."

"Thank goodness," J. Aubrey said with breathless sincerity.

THIRTY-ONE

J. AUBREY'S FACE fell and with it all his hopes and aspirations for this . . . place.

San Antonio was no city. Except, perhaps, by Texas standards.

It was little better than a village. And a foreign-looking village at that. Houses made of mud. Public buildings, what few of them there were, made of mud. Why, the people here had so little pride that they even allowed the ruins of some falling-apart old church to stand—with its mud walls, of course—practically adjacent to the miserable, muddy little village. It looked like an old mission church, but now the roof had collapsed and the walls were deeply pocked and pitted by the ravages of time and vandals. The old mission now looked more a refugee than a refuge.

"That's the Alamo," Squint Hay said as he held his horse close beside the rolling, bouncing wagon.

J. Aubrey sniffed. Whatever these rustics chose to call the silly thing, it was undeniably an eyesore. A community with any sense of pride in itself would have torn the ugly old structure down years ago.

"We'll be losing some of our people here. Couple them carts was only wanting t' go this far," Hay went on.

"Whyever would they have wanted to wait for a train to be made up if they were only coming this far?" Pollack asked from the seat beside J. Aubrey's at the fore of the small wagon.

"Safety in numbers," Hay said. "If the Injuns is raiding this year. But don' you worry none. We'll likely pick us up some more folks here t' go with us t' El Paso del Norte."

"I thought there was no threat of Indians here," J. Aubrey injected.

"Mostly there ain't," Hay agreed. "But a fella never knows.

Anyhow, it ain't here that we're fixing t' stay, you know. We get out past Fredericksburg, the country gets kinda empty. Might roll all the way to Californy without seeing a Injun. Might go five mile an' run into a bushel of 'em. Best t' not take no chances."

"Are all the residents here Mexican?"

"Nope." Hay turned his head and spat a stream of yellow tobacco juice. "Just most of 'em. Something wrong 'bout that?"

"No," J. Aubrey said quickly. "Not a thing." It occurred to him that he knew little about Mexicans, other than that their language was incomprehensible and that they smiled a great deal. Likely they would be gullible enough. They might even have banks of sorts. On the other hand, they all seemed too poor to buy decent clothing for themselves. Grown men went around in daytime wearing white pajamas instead of proper suits. There would be no point in trying to make his score here.

"Hotel's right over there," Hay said, pointing.

At least that was still something a gentleman could look forward to. Hay had mentioned something about a bath, hadn't he.

The passenger wagons were directed to the hotel—it was, predictably, made of the same dreary mud as everything else—and Hay guided the remainder of the train out of sight to the south.

J. Aubrey took a moment to stretch his limbs, then gathered up his expeditioners like a mother hen gathering in her chicks. "I shall make our arrangements, gentlemen, fear not."

Which was somewhat easier promised than done.

The inside of the inn—Capt. Hay might choose to term it a hotel; J. Aubrey would hardly consider it such—was dark and cool behind the thick mud walls. The Mexican who seemed to be in charge spoke English. Fortunately.

"I represent the Whitford Expedition. No doubt you anticipated our arrival." J. Aubrey introduced himself with an immodest flourish.

"How many?" the innkeeper demanded, seemingly unimpressed with the honor he was being paid by the presence of the Whitford Expedition.

"Twenty ni . . . , um, no, make that thirty. That's right. Thirty persons. My expedition members, however, can double up in their accommodations. Naturally I shall require a private room for myself. And an immediate bath, my good man." J. Aubrey removed his top hat and placed it onto the counter with a proprietary air. He smiled at the clerk, then dipped his eyes to examine the state of his fingernails. A manicure might be in order, he thought, in addition to the bath. Provided, perhaps, by a fetching Mexican miss.

"I got six rooms, señor. No bath. There is tub at barber place, two blocks down."

"Six . . . rooms."

The Mexican smiled and nodded. "Six rooms, six dollars. Bath is five cents. Don' let that t'ief Ramirez charge you more. Five cents, no more."

"Six rooms," J. Aubrey said again. Weakly.

"Sí. Very clean, very nice. You want all o' them, señor?"

J. Aubrey shuddered. "Yes, I shall acquire all six if you please."

The inn clerk grinned and nodded and accepted his payment in advance.

THIRTY-TWO

J. AUBREY had to assume responsibility for herding all the expeditioners down to the barber shop and arranging the five-cent baths. He supposed he would have to arrange for the evening meal as well. There hadn't been any sign of Squint Hay since the little man took the wagon train off a while ago.

The leader of the Whitford Expedition had quite frankly been hoping that not all his people would be interested in bathing this evening. Aside from the expense, there was the bother of it all. But virtually everyone, including Smith and his spuriously named cronies, wanted to come along.

Now they were all lined up underneath the shelter of a mud and sapling porch roof, outside the barber's place of business. The only thing remotely familiar on this entire street, J. Aubrey reflected, was the striped barber pole that had been painted onto one of the porch roof's upright support posts. Except for that homey little touch they might all have been a thousand miles from civilization.

Come to think of it, J. Aubrey realized, they *were* a thousand miles from any real civilization. Possibly further. He scowled and talked with "the thief Ramirez."

"Ten cents each bath," Ramirez told him.

"The regular price is five cents," J. Aubrey said firmly. "And I expect a quantity price reduction below that. Take a look outside, if you please. I shall pay three cents. Not a single penny more."

Ramirez looked outside. And smiled. Unfortunately the man seemed to have a monopoly on washtubs in this vicinity. He refused to budge below five cents. And insisted he would be able to change the bath water no more than twice at that price, pleading some silliness about a lack of hot water as his excuse.

"I've arranged our ablutions, gentlemen," J. Aubrey announced. "I suggest a limit of three minutes per bath or we shall be here half the night."

J. Aubrey was no fool. He left the other members of the Baja expedition standing outside and hurried to make himself the first of the many bathers. The thought of being the tenth man in line to use that same tepid bath water . . .

When he returned to the patio, if such it could be called, to beckon the next in line, he discovered that the expeditioners had discovered an amusement by which they could pass the time whilst they waited for the tub.

The activity was one with which J. Aubrey was entirely familiar, San Antonio being a foreign sort of place or not, but despite that familiarity he felt his stomach knot and churn.

How *dare* some penny-ante Mexican sharper move in on a gentleman's marks?

Why, J. Aubrey hadn't nursed these fellows across half a continent just to allow someone else to clean them out beneath his very own nose. No, indeed, he had not.

He squared his shoulders and shot his chin and marched up to the tiny table that had been brought into place while J. Aubrey was enjoying his bath.

The Mexican scammer was heartless. Unimaginative too. Although he'd at least had sense enough to select a play that was tried and true.

The rascal had three nutshell halves laid cupped side down atop the smooth planed tabletop and was running a classic shell game.

The Mexican's only departure from tradition was that he was using pecan shells instead of the traditional walnut halves.

J. Aubrey Whitford, however, was a fair-minded man. He gave credit where it was properly due, and he had to admire the dexterity of anyone who would use shells with an exterior as smooth as pecan in place of the much rougher texture available with walnut.

J. Aubrey watched only for a short while.

Smith, who with his friends had bulled close to the head of the bath line, was placing bets as large as two bits, and half a dozen others were adding to the play by making their own side bets to Smith's selection of the shell.

Why, there was well over a dollar being extracted from the pockets of the expeditioners with every shuffle.

The grinning Mexican scammer—who seemed to speak no English but found that to be no handicap—was well in clover.

J. Aubrey observed as the Mexican placed a perfectly ordinary dried pea onto the tabletop. Clapped a shell-half down over it. Placed the two empty shells to the left of the one containing the pea everyone had seen go down there. Then began to scrape the shells with swift dexterity back and forth and side to side.

The excitement among the Americans was high.

"I got it. I see it," Smith declared loudly. "I know which'un it is, boys." He sounded pleased. He pointed.

The Mexican, still grinning, lifted the pecan shell.

J. Aubrey grunted an acknowledgment of the man's skill. The Mexican was as smart as he was dexterous. The pea was there, right where Smith said it should be. The Mexican smiled and paid over his losses.

Huh! Of course. Keep the marks eager. The smart scammer knows that. Always give your mark hope enough to make him greedy for more.

The Mexican motioned toward his movable table, and the company of expeditioners practically fell over themselves in their hurry to lay more money down.

J. Aubrey scowled at the Mexican for a moment, then turned and walked away.

It would do no good to try and explain anything to the expeditioners. Besides, it's never a good idea to educate a mark. Some things simply aren't done.

And there were better ways to handle this.

J. Aubrey yawned and stopped into a store on the same block, looked about for a moment and wandered on. He had to investigate three others before he found what he wanted.

Then, hands in pockets, he ambled back the way he had come, and once again joined the throng outside the barber shop. He heard a groan of disappointment as he came near.

"Again," Smith said loudly. "I'll go again, dammit."

The Mexican shrugged, smiled, laid the pea down and covered it with a nutshell. His hands began to dart and slide and shift about with a slyly deceptive speed.

J. Aubrey edged into the crowd and reached Smith's side.

Smith, his face a study in frowning concentration, pointed a grimy forefinger at the pecan shell to his right.

The Mexican stoically lifted the shell. And collected his winnings from the side of the table.

"Damn!" Smith mumbled.

"I do believe it's your turn in the tub," J. Aubrey said although he had no idea whose place was the next in line.

"I wanta get even," Smith snarled.

"Of course, but I suspect the gentleman shall be here as long as any of us wishes to play. Why don't I take your place at the table while you bathe, eh? You'll only be a few minutes."

Smith grudgingly assented.

"Excuse me, please. Let me get a good view here," J. Aubrey said politely.

Enough of the expeditioners shuffled aside to give him room.

J. Aubrey pointed at his own chest, then down to the table. The Mexican smiled again. J. Aubrey smiled back at him. Coins were placed down, although fewer of them than had been laid to back Smith's guesswork. But then Smith, after all, had already demonstrated an early ability to disclose the errant pea. Surely it was only luck that had kept him from doing so more recently. The expeditioners were as yet unsure of their leader's ability to do as well with this little game.

The pea was placed. The shells swerved and circled. The Mexican, satisfied, lined all three into a tidy row. He smiled.

J. Aubrey frowned in deep concentration. He scowled. He tilted his head this way and then that. He reached forward, hesitated, allowed his hand to hover above this shell and then that one. Someone behind him groaned.

"I believe there is a one in three chance no matter what shell is selected, mmm?" J. Aubrey said to no one in particular.

The Mexican smiled.

J. Aubrey reached down. Before the Mexican knew what he was about, J. Aubrey lifted one of the pecan shells. It was just as well that his hands were clean and his fingers limber. As he'd expected, the pecan shell was much more difficult to play than walnut.

Still, the pea was where he'd "guessed" it to be.

The Mexican blinked. And for the first time frowned.

J. Aubrey smiled at him. And picked up his winnings.

"Care to go again, old fellow?" J. Aubrey invited.

The Mexican said something that was loud and sharp and quite rapidly uttered. Very probably it was quite a good thing that no one in this crowd spoke any Spanish, or J. Aubrey might have felt obligated to defend his honor with the cheeky fellow.

J. Aubrey laid a five-dollar gold piece on the edge of the table.

The Mexican snapped out some more rapid-fire Spanish and pushed the wager away, refusing the play. He pocketed his pea —or more accurately, J. Aubrey's pea—and his shells and grabbed up the little table.

"Hey," some expeditioner protested. "You can't do that."

"Mr. Whitford was just gettin' warmed up," somebody else said.

"Come back here, damn you."

The Mexican ignored the gentlemen and hurried away.

J. Aubrey kept pace with him for a few yards. Just long enough to get a glare of disapproval that J. Aubrey answered with a wink.

"Those gentlemen are private property," J. Aubrey explained. "But it is a shame I had to break it up for you. You are really very good. Pity you don't understand me. I wish I could tell you how much I admire your work."

"Thank you, señor," the Mexican said in English quite as

good as that of nearly anyone else in Texas. "You are almos' as good as me, eh? You put that pea down very nice. Even I didn' see you do it. Not that I was looking for it, eh? Who would have thought. But you are very good. Almos' as good as Carlos." He thumped himself on his chest by way of introduction when he spoke the name.

J. Aubrey laughed. "Good luck to you, Carlos. Please stay away from my people, and I'll not interfere again."

Carlos chuckled and winked.

J. Aubrey turned back to his expeditioners. Who still, thank goodness, had most of their cash in their own pockets.

He didn't really begrudge the fact that they had a few dollars less now than they'd had a little while ago.

After all, skill like Carlos's deserved reward. And there hadn't been all that much extracted.

III

The Girl

THIRTY-THREE

"YOU'LL LIKE FREDERICKSBURG," Squint Hay said.

"Oh?" J. Aubrey recalled that the man had said much the same about San Antonio. That left room for considerable doubt as pertained to Fredericksburg.

"Yeah, I think so. Settled by a bunch o' Germans. Make a helluva sausage there, they do. It always wonders me that all Germans ain't fat. Me, I'd puff up like a toad if I could get some o' them sausages every day." He laughed and settled for a chew —"chaw," they called it here—off his plug in lieu of a bite of Fredericksburg sausage.

"How far is it?"

"Four days or thereabouts."

"From here?"

"From San Antone."

Which meant they should be roughly halfway to the German community now. On the second day out from San Antonio the wagons were rolling through limestone-studded hills that were sheathed in short grasses and liberally dotted with small cedars. This was a fair land watered by small rivers and smaller streams. The comments from the expeditioners were favorable, particularly from those members who had been farmers before they became seekers of golden fortune.

"Are there decent hotel accommodations in Fredericksburg?" J. Aubrey asked. It still rankled him that the inn in San Antonio had been so disappointing.

"Wasn't none the last time I come through," Hay told him. "I hear tell, though, that there's been a new hotel built. Nice place, they say. You'd best hope so 'cause we'll lay up in Fredericksburg a couple days t' see to the wagons afore we head west. Bad country out there, y'see. You want t' have your rigs tended to before you put Fredericksburg behind. 'Sides, there ain't another regular hotel 'tween there an' California.''

J. Aubrey sat upright on the wagon seat and sent a skeptical look about him. He sniffed.

Squint Hay might call this bad country. But then Squint Hay was a man who chose to live amid the barren ugliness of the coastal plains, where there was hardly a tree to be seen from one horizon to the next, and where everything that lived had either stickers or stingers.

This country, in contrast, might hold few people, but it was a much softer and more agreeable land than was back near the coast.

Probably, J. Aubrey decided, Mr. Hay was fearful of the likelihood of Indian attack out here away from settlement.

And after all, the people back in San Antonio said it had been many years since the Indians raided there. Many of them were of the belief that the Indians were no longer any threat in Texas.

J. Aubrey preferred to accept their judgment on the subject, particularly as they, and not Mr. Hay, resided farther to the west.

J. Aubrey swiveled about on the seat and peered down the length of the dusty column.

It was much longer now than when they had left Victoria. As Hay predicted, they'd lost most of the Mexican *carretas* at San Antonio, but those had been replaced and then some. There were also several other freight wagons in the train now, traders with goods to transport out to distant El Paso del Norte, several families who for some reason chose to relocate so far from civilized comfort. There were more livestock in the trailing herds too, and mules and milk cattle and even a flock of hairy goats. There had been men wanting to send oxen west with the expedition, but Hay refused them, as they were too slow for the pace he wanted to maintain.

J. Aubrey frankly did not care a fig about the rest of the train. If these Germans at Fredericksburg had a bank—Germans are a prosperous people, are they not?—J. Aubrey's personal interest in the train might well terminate there.

Goodness, he certainly hoped so.

He faced forward again and gave thought to their arrival in Fredericksburg two days hence.

THIRTY-FOUR

THIS WAS MORE LIKE IT. Why, this was *much* more like it.

Fredericksburg was a town of orderly streets and gingerbread houses. These were sidewalks before the businesses and a bandstand on the square. Most of all, there was paint, white paint, on the wooden walls. J. Aubrey had seen hardly anything in the way of painted structures since he made his esca—since he left New York.

Squint Hay led the train on toward a wagon park he knew of, but detailed the passenger rigs carrying the Whitford Expedition directly to the hotel. J. Aubrey was smiling all the way. At last, even here in Texas, there was civilization.

"Marvelous," J. Aubrey uttered as the creaky mud wagon crunched and groaned to a halt outside the tall, white-painted Nimitz Hotel on Washington. That little touch amused him. Washington, Jefferson; the Germans might have named their community after a foreign princeling, but their streets were given patriotic American names, presumably to honor their new country. The street intersecting Washington where the new Nimitz stood was called Main. Change the foliage just a little and Fredericksburg might have been any small town in New England.

J. Aubrey waited for the Mexican driver to scramble down and help him to descend, then brushed off his lapels and saw to the state of his hat before he presented himself with chin high inside the Nimitz.

"J. Aubrey Whitford, sir. At your service." He swept the hat off and bowed low to the stocky German, slightly short of middle years, who attended the counter there. "You have heard of me, of course."

"Charles Nimitz," the man said, returning the bow with a bob of his head. "You wish rooms?"

"I wish rooms," J. Aubrey agreed. "I am leading an expedition of thirty persons to the Baja lands. We shall be here two, perhaps three nights. We require accommodations and a bath. Most particularly a bath."

"Of course." Nimitz bowed again. The man's accent was thick but his English comprehensible enough. He didn't sound like anyone who should be named Charles. But then J. Aubrey had no quarrel with a man who might find reason to alter his name.

A deal was soon struck. Board included. J. Aubrey was satisfied, even though his supply of ready cash was too quickly evaporating. At the moment that hardly mattered. These Germans were sure to have a bank. And a gentleman must show a front if he expects to profit. This was not a time for penury.

J. Aubrey rubbed his palms together with glad anticipation, as the bags and bundles were carted within and the members of the expedition shown to their rooms.

Tomorrow, he thought. Tomorrow it would all fall together, and this entire experience could be put behind him.

Tomorrow—he had been thinking about little else since leaving San Antonio—tomorrow he would insist on resupplying the expeditioners for the remainder of the journey west. That would require cash payment to the burghers of Fredericksburg. It would be in the expeditioners' best interest to see that the gentleman's bank drafts were honored. And with both their support and that of Capt. Hay, why, there should be no problem whatsoever in achieving the conversion J. Aubrey required.

THIRTY-FIVE

"THAT'S DAMN NICE o' you, Aubrey, but you don't understand the way we do things hereabouts," Squint Hay said around a mouthful of sausage. Which was, J. Aubrey had to admit, quite as good as promised.

" 'Side from you not needin' t' try an' help me out," Hay was saying, "I already got the wagon repairs tooken care of." The suggestion had been that the Whitford Expedition provide for maintenance of the Hay wagons, in light of the fact that this trip was being undertaken on their behalf. The rest of that truth, of course, was that J. Aubrey wanted as many merchants as possible interested in seeing a successful bank transaction concluded by Mr. Whitford.

"Four o' them cows I brought was brought just for this. Two each t' the smith an' the wheelwright. Good men. I know 'em. They'll take my cows in trade for the work. Works out good. I can git the cows for nothin' but the trouble o' catchin' them. Hepner an' Samuels get meat an' hides for their labor. Ain't no cash money needed. Most things is like that here 'cause we ain't heavy on cash money. We kinda trade about." He swallowed and immediately stuffed another chunk of hot, greasy, delicious sausage into his face. "Just you let me worry 'bout such, Aubrey. I got 'er covered."

"But I insist . . ."

"Nope, dang it, I done told you. Now leave be, Aubrey." Squint Hay concentrated his attentions on the meal, the subject obviously closed so far as he was concerned.

It was something J. Aubrey supposed he could live with. Just so long as he was able to run up a bill with the grocers sufficiently large as to require the conversion of a draft. Or several. He would, of course, manage. He always did. He smiled and tried to devote himself to the best meal he'd had at least since the barbecue back in Victoria.

"I don't want to rush anyone, but there is a second seating waiting for dis table, gentlemen."

J. Aubrey frowned, but Squint Hay seemed unaffected by the prompting. The lean Texan's plate was already empty for the second or third time, while J. Aubrey was barely finishing his first helping. Even so, J. Aubrey couldn't resist another bit of the potatoes in a sour dressing, and another slab of sausage that he wrapped in white bread. How long had it been since he'd last tasted white bread?

"Come along, Aubrey. We'll go inta the salon an' have a nip."

"As you wish, Mr. Hay."

Hay gave him a mournful look.

"Sorry. As you wish, Squint." The familiarity did not come easy to J. Aubrey's tongue. Hay, however, grinned, apparently as pleased as if he'd just been complimented. He took J. Aubrey by the elbow and guided him, still chewing, out of the dining room past the other expeditioners who were gathered in the lobby waiting for second seating.

The salon was a tiny affair situated across the lobby from the dining room. It held an assortment of mismatched chairs and a plumply upholstered sofa. There was a small writing desk with paper, ink and cheap pens—J. Aubrey gave the stamped steel pens a disdainful glance—and a low table containing ragged newspapers and long out-of-date periodicals in both English and German.

"Have yourself a sit, Aubrey. I'll see if I can't promote us some brandy," Hay said with a wink and a nod.

"Very kind of you, I'm sure," J. Aubrey said, hiding a belch behind his hand. The sausage tasted almost as good this second time as it had the first.

Hay disappeared into the lobby. The other expeditioners who had been at the first seating were already on their way upstairs to their rooms. For the time being J. Aubrey had the salon to himself. He settled into an armchair and looked over the reading materials. There was nothing that interested him.

Out in the lobby, however, there was something that interested him very much indeed.

A young woman had entered and was standing at the counter talking with Mr. Nimitz.

The lady was *most* fetching. And it wasn't only the amount of time J. Aubrey'd had to spend in wholly masculine company that prompted him to believe so. He was sure of that. This woman would have turned heads on Fifth Avenue.

She was of diminutive height but excellent proportion. This he could see quite well, as she was standing in profile to him. She wore a rather plain gown of a medium gray shade, but lent the simple garment quality by way of her own force of character. Her bearing if not her wardrobe was elegant. She had golden hair curled into the style known as "cats, rats, and mice"; three rolls of differing sizes draped across her pretty scalp. And her face, ah. J. Aubrey stared undetected as the lady conferred with Charles Nimitz.

Nimitz said something to her, listened for a moment and nodded twice in response to something she said. Then he smiled and came out from behind his counter to catch Squint Hay by the elbow as the rugged little Texan returned from his errand, with two glasses in hand and a bulge in his coat pocket.

Hay paused, then smiled also. He stood where he was, brandy glasses and mission forgotten, while the handsome young woman spoke to him.

At length Hay nodded, and the young lady's face brightened with pleasure.

She turned and hurried outside the hotel. Hay said something more to Nimitz, and the German shrugged. Hay finally remembered the reason why he was standing there with two glasses and a flask. He said something to Nimitz and returned, finally, to the salon.

But he did not, darn him, say anything to J. Aubrey about the young beauty who had just approached him.

THIRTY-SIX

THIS WAS A SHOPPING SPREE the like of which J. Aubrey had never experienced before. And certainly not in such quantities.

He ordered hundredweight sacks of flour, fine ground corn-meal and rice. Tin buckets of lard and sealed tins of saleratus. Casks of vinegar and crates of heavily salted bacon. A barrel of salt pork and a keg of salted cod. It seemed superfluous but he also bought salt in huge quantity.

He tried to buy casks of whiskey and discovered that that was not the way things were done when traveling here. Here one transported grain alcohol by the keg and converted it into whis-key as needed, by the addition of water and assorted other dilutants, coloring syrups and flavorings, in order to create an approximation of whiskey.

That was fine by J. Aubrey. It allowed him to shop for just that many more items.

The merchants of Fredericksburg loved him. And he loved them, bless their hearts. J. Aubrey took considerable pains to spread his business among all.

By the end of the day he had run up tabs totaling several hundreds of dollars.

The actual merchandise he neither saw nor—if the truth be known—cared about. The goods would all be delivered to the Hay wagon train at the park on the stream nearby. The mer-chants would see to all of that. All Mr. Whitford need do was pay in full.

J. Aubrey smiled and contained himself.

There was a bank in Fredericksburg. He has ascertained that to begin with. It was a small affair attached to the pharmacy. He was sure it was quite perfect. These Germans were falling all over themselves in their eagerness to do business with the handsome and prosperous gentleman who had come into their midst as the leader of a daring expedition.

Ah, but he would not approach the bank. Not yet. Not today.

A certain amount of judicious restraint must be maintained if one expects to achieve a score worthy of the game.

Tonight the cafes and the beer parlors, the card rooms and the practice halls—the Germans of Fredericksburg seemed quite addicted to their beer and their music—would be abuzz with talk about the well-made gentleman from New York and his free spending habits.

By morning the whole community would be aware of the amount of cash being injected into their economy by Mr. J. Aubrey Whitford and his expeditioners.

And by tomorrow morning as well, the fat German banker— J. Aubrey quite expected the man to be precisely that, and perhaps a trifle soft-headed to boot—would be eager to participate in the good fortune that was befalling his fellow townsmen.

By tomorrow morning J. Aubrey expected the banker to be willing to come to him with suggestions for the care of Whitford's fortunes.

But, considerately, J. Aubrey intended to save the fellow the trouble.

J. Aubrey ate heartily that evening, but enjoyed something less than his fair share of the beer and brandy to be had afterward. He intended to have a clear head and steady hand come the morrow.

THIRTY-SEVEN

"ACH, THE HERR WHITFORD, ja. Come in, come in." The welcome was every bit as warm as J. Aubrey'd hoped. The banker's name was Kimmel. The gilt lettering on his door gave his initial as *M,* whatever that might stand for.

J. Aubrey smiled and accepted Kimmel's offered hand. He allowed himself to be shown into the glass-fronted cubicle that served as the bank president's office. J. Aubrey was at his natty best today in freshly brushed outer clothing, freshly laundered —thanks to the services of the hotel—boiled shirt and freshly starched and ironed collar. His tall and handsome hat he had attended himself. He felt fresh and vigorous and very much in charge now.

M. Kimmel was not exactly J. Aubrey's idea of what a German banker should be, but he would do. Instead of being plump and graying and bristling with mustaches, Kimmel was a lean and saturnine fellow with dark hair and pale eyes. Not a day more than thirty, J. Aubrey guessed. Which could work quite nicely to the good, especially if this Kimmel was the spoiled son of wealthy burgher parentage, who maintained himself by playing at being a banker. Very much to the good indeed if that were so. J. Aubrey decided immediately to adopt a man-of-the world posture here. Overwhelm this backwoods bookkeeper with a cosmopolitan air and strike for all that was available.

J. Aubrey sent a surreptitious glance toward the safe that resided in a corner of Kimmel's office.

There was no vault in the place, only the squat little EverTite. And it wasn't even chained in place. Trusting souls these burghers of Fredericksburg. Why, J. Aubrey had acquaintances who could roll the front off an EverTite easy as peeling an apple and perhaps more quickly. Not, of course, that that was J. Aubrey

Whitford's forte. Theft was so . . . disagreeable. Still and all . . .

J. Aubrey coughed into his fist while Kimmel proceeded through the customary pleasantries.

He was busy trying to calculate how much coin a smallish EverTite might reasonably contain. Not a great deal to be sure. But far more than anyone might expect to encounter farther west.

J. Aubrey smiled.

"I understand, Herr Whitford, that you require the services of this bank, ja?"

"You understand correctly, sir." Good. The information had been spreading through the community exactly as desired.

"And the nature of this service, Herr Whitford?"

An inspiration came to him in one glorious leap. A stroke of purest genius. It was enough to make J. Aubrey flush with pleasure in appreciation of his own talents.

"A deposit, sir," J. Aubrey said easily, abandoning most of his carefully thought-out plan and substituting a better one on this spur of the moment.

It was Kimmel's turn to smile. And no wonder. What banker can ever resist the allure of new deposits.

"A trifling sum to be sure, sir," J. Aubrey said negligently, "but nonetheless . . ." He made a depreciatory gesture with his left hand and with his right withdrew from his coat pocket the sheaf of remaining "drafts" against the First Continental Bank of New York. "I've been talking with Capt. Hay, you understand, and he tells me that your establishment will be the closest and most reliable such institution to the scene of our endeavors in distant Baja."

"Ach, of course," Kimmel agreed. He smiled. J. Aubrey smiled.

"Naturally I am concerned about the security of my deposits. Capt. Hay tells me, as do the merchants of your fair community, that my funds will be safe with you, sir." It never hurt to dab a tot of butter onto the mark before one skins him—helps the hide to slide off more easily.

"Safe, ja, I assure you."

"I am prepared to deposit with you, sir, the bulk of my expedition's assets." J. Aubrey smoothed his self-made draft certificates atop Kimmel's desk, paused for a moment while he pretended to consider and then judiciously retrieved one of them and returned it to his inner pocket. "Subject, of course, to withdrawal and transfer to whatever point required."

"Yes, just so," Kimmel agreed.

"Naturally I haven't decided yet what to do about my personal assets. I may choose to transfer them here as well, depending on the success of our venture in the Baja, sir."

Kimmel nodded sagely, leaned back in a creaking swivel chair and knitted his fingers together over his chain and fob. "We"—it sounded more like *ve*—"vould be glad to serve you, Herr Whitford."

"Capital. I knew I could count on you, sir. Your community holds you in the highest regard. I see that their faith is well founded."

Kimmel smiled again.

"I shall place on deposit with you seven thousand dollars, drawn against the First Continental in New York City. You may have heard of it?"

"Ja, I know it vell."

"Excellent, sir. As I said, I shall deposit seven thousand with you by way of drafts, then draw back funds sufficient to see us through to El Paso del Norte and on to the Baja. Capt. Hay tells me it may be difficult to negotiate drafts west of here. He suggests some cash be carried despite the risks inherent." J. Aubrey reached for the quill and ink bottle that rested on a corner of Kimmel's desk. "I hope, sir, it will be convenient for you to receive raw gold from us and convert it to specie once our, um, mining endeavors begin to generate returns?"

"Most convenient, ja. This I can do for you also," Kimmel said.

"Bully, sir. I just knew we'd found our man when I heard about you." He shook his head. "I can't tell you how I've worried about this aspect of our adventure. So far from home and all my normal banking contacts, you understand. It has fair driven me gray with worry, ha ha." He ran a hand through his mane of thick and ungrayed hair.

Kimmel smiled tightly.

The banker leaned forward, accepted the draft certificates and turned them about so he could the better examine them.

Examination was a precaution J. Aubrey welcomed. The certificates were, after all, the product of truly exquisite craftsmanship. J. Aubrey was proud of them to the point that he had no fear of close perusal. He leaned back in his own hard-bottomed chair and waited patiently.

Kimmel looked, grunted, nodded. A moment later the banker frowned. He looked up with an eyebrow cocked.

"Yes?" J. Aubrey asked.

"The name on this certificate, Herr Whitford."

"Yes, my signature. You can see it right there. And of course to be signed again to verify it against my countersignature on that line right down . . . ," he leaned closer and pointed, "down there." It was to be expected. A small-time banker like this Kimmel fellow possibly never before saw such a certificate. At least not from a bank so exalted as the First Continental.

"No, no," Kimmel said quickly. "Your signature, ja, I see there. But this one is what I mean." He pointed.

J. Aubrey shrugged. "That line was signed by an officer of the bank in New York, sir. I forget his name and title. But then, sir, I hadn't the pleasure of meeting the man. A junior officer presented the certificates to me after issue."

Actually J. Aubrey had scant fear about that point either. And he knew both name and title quite well even though it was true enough that the gentleman and he were not socially acquainted. Monvil P. Munk, vice president. J. Aubrey long since researched the name and title—he preferred to leave nothing to chance—and had been using both quite happily ever since.

"But this is most irregular, Herr Whitford."

"How so?"

"I know Herr Munk. He has become senior vice president since last September. I remember this very well. I sent him myself the note of congratulation, you understand. These certificates should have been signed by Herr Carter who is now in that position. Herr Carter too I know although not so vell as Herr Munk."

"How odd," J. Aubrey agreed smoothly. He smiled again. Shrugged. "Oh well. Filling in at the old stand for some reason? I wouldn't know, sir. Don't know either of the gentlemen, you see. I only know that I deposited gold into my personal accounts there and secured drafts for the purposes of travel with my expedition. On the advice, I might add, of a teller at the First Continental."

"Of course. It was excellent advice, Herr Whitford. But even so, I must wonder . . . you would not mind, perhaps, if I take these certificates to show to my father?"

"I would not mind at all," J. Aubrey assured him.

The banker's tiny office certainly lacked for ventilation. It seemed rather warm within. J. Aubrey maintained his outward composure, however, and continued to smile.

"My father's health does not permit him to spend regular hours here, Herr Whitford. I may, perhaps, take these certificates to him?"

"Certainly."

"Then we should meet again after lunch?"

"Whatever you wish," J. Aubrey said with an air of unconcern. "Tomorrow if you like. No, wait. Capt. Hay said our party may be free to leave in the morning if the wheelwright has all the spokes tightened by that time. This afternoon might be better after all."

"Two o'clock, Herr Whitford?"

"That would be fine." J. Aubrey stood, shook the extended hand, then made his way slowly and with dignity out through a bank lobby not much larger than this stuffy little office.

THIRTY-EIGHT

J. AUBREY'S STRIDE lengthened once he was free of the confinements of that damned hicksville bank. He hurried back to the Nimitz and straight up to his room. Beneath his coat the shirt was sopping, and a brief examination in a mirror showed that his collar was wilting as well. Damn that Kimmel anyway. Whoever would have expected . . . Besides, who would expect a bank to change its personnel so freely? Could a man trust in nothing any longer? This entire situation was becoming most disagreeable.

He stripped to his waist and took the opportunity to pour a little cool water into the crockery basin and wash, then dressed once again in fresh linen and selected a new collar. Thank goodness he had another available. The shopping he'd done since leaving his things behind in New York was paying off now. It wouldn't do to turn up at Kimmel's office after dinner wearing an inferior celluloid collar or, heaven forbid, one of those enameled steel contraptions. There were some things that a gentleman simply did not do. Besides, it wouldn't be wise at this point to make that damned Kimmel think Herr Whitford had been sweating.

Refreshed and feeling himself again, J. Aubrey went down to the hotel dining room. A few of the expeditioners were there. So were Squint Hay and the fetching young woman J. Aubrey'd noticed the previous evening. A twinge of jealousy touched J. Aubrey when he saw the scrawny Texan—who was securely married, as their conversations of the recent past disclosed—dining at the same table as the pretty young lady.

"Aubrey," Hay said, beckoning when he saw the expedition leader enter, "whyn't you join us?"

"With pleasure." He bowed low before the blonde lady.

"Aubrey Whitford, this here's Miss Grace Woolrich," Hay drawled, getting the introduction quite bollixed up, although no real harm was done. "Miss Grace, this's the gennelman I was tellin' you about."

J. Aubrey held himself stiffly erect and bowed once more, considerably lower this time. Miss Woolrich—not missus, he was pleased to note; the married ones are seldom promiscuous so young—extended her hand, and J. Aubrey touched his finger-tips to it. "I am honored, miss. Particularly so to meet one so aptly named as yourself, if I may be so bold." Mmm. The speech was not so pretty as it might have been. Too many so's, he realized even as he finished the sentence.

Miss Woolrich didn't seem to mind. She chuckled a little and inclined her lovely head in the direction of an empty chair between hers and Squint Hay's.

"Thank you."

"Mr. Hay has been telling me about your expedition, Mr. Whitford. I must say it sounds exciting. To think that you may discover gold in Old Mexico."

"Adventure is its own reward, Miss Woolrich. The prospect of fabulous wealth merely heightens one's anticipation. Although they do say that this find may be the source of all the riches of ancient Spain."

"I thought the wealth of the *conquistadores*"—her pronunciation of the word had a decidedly Spanish twist to the tongue—"was in silver and slaves, Mr. Whitford."

"Only partially," J. Aubrey assured her, with no idea whatsoever how a bunch of long-dead Spaniards had enriched themselves.

"How interesting," the girl enthused. "Perhaps you would tell me more on the subject, Mr. Whitford?"

"It would be my pleasure, Miss Woolrich."

And *that* was the bedrock truth. If only he could find a way now to ease Squint Hay off to tend to his duties somewhere . . .

"Miss Grace's gonna be traveling with us, Aubrey," Hay put

in as if by divine providence. J. Aubrey felt his chest swell. "She's wantin' t' go on with us t' El Paso del Norte."

"Have you your own vehicle, Miss Woolrich? If not I should be honored to have you ride as a guest in my wagon." Someone —McArdle, perhaps; the man didn't bathe nearly often enough for the riding comfort of his fellow travelers—could be shunted off into another wagon in order to make room for so fair a companion.

One thing J. Aubrey was sure of. No one in the lead wagon would complain about the change, save McArdle himself.

"I accept your hospitality, sir," the charming young woman said.

"Mr. Hay? Squint, I mean?"

Hay shrugged. "It don't make no nevermind t' me, Aubrey. You folks do as y' please."

Oh my, yes, J. Aubrey thought gladly.

Except of course, he suddenly realized, he wouldn't be with the wagon train after today.

Not if Kimmel and his miserable father accepted those draft certificates.

Which they surely would do within the hour.

J. Aubrey sighed.

Why must it be that blessings are so very often tinged with sadness.

Still, a gentleman must do what a gentleman must do. And there wouldn't be need after all to send poor McArdle off to another wagon. Miss Woolrich could occupy J. Aubrey's own position on the forward seat once he decamped. Probably she would end up married to Pollack or Bolliger or some other such. A waste, that was what that would be. But of course it had to be done.

J. Aubrey smiled. "What fare do you recommend from the menu today, Miss Woolrich?"

THIRTY-NINE

J. AUBREY took his time over dinner, lingering with pie and coffee while he enjoyed the pleasure of Miss Woolrich's company. He was in no hurry. Far from it, in fact. Apart from the grace and beauty of Miss Grace, it never pays to seem in a hurry when one waits for a well-laid snare to close. It simply wouldn't do for him to make his appearance back at the bank too quickly. A few minutes before the normal closing hour should be about right, he judged.

He smiled and presented himself at his charming best to the young lady. If only there were more time . . .

The girl was quite . . . remarkable. Pretty. Well-read. Able to turn a phrase or make a rhyme. Certainly able to turn a head. Poor Hay was far out of his depth. The conversation flowed above him like a sun-brightened cloud over a dry and thorny Texas prairie. The fellow excused himself early and left the field to the oratory and the wit of J. Aubrey Whitford alone. J. Aubrey did not mind, nor did the young lady seem to. J. Aubrey preened. Chuckled. Charmed. He very nearly sat through the remainder of the day's banking hours, he was enjoying himself so thoroughly.

"If you would excuse me, Miss Woolrich?" he reluctantly said at length. "It is only the press of business that requires me to leave. Perhaps we could resume our conversation later? Over dinner?"

Her smile was shy. But accompanied by a nod of her blonde head. "It would be my pleasure, Mr. Whitford."

J. Aubrey beamed. He retrieved his hat. Paused in the lobby foyer to examine his collar and tie in a poorly silvered mirror. Impeccable. The only thing he lacked was a walking stick. By all means he should acquire one forthwith, just as soon as his bank drafts were cashed. Assuming a suitable accessory could be found here, of course.

He was in high spirits as he strolled toward the tiny, backwater bank of Fredericksburg.

"Sir?" J. Aubrey frowned, his posture quite nearly as stiff as his expression now. "Am I to assume, sir, that you do not wish to undertake my banking affairs?"

"You misunderstand me, Herr Whitford. That is not at all what you should assume, please." Kimmel hadn't even the good grace to look apologetic about this. His demeanor was solemn but not at all bending. "It would be our pleasure to receive your deposits and to make disbursements however you require. It is only that we must first to clear the drafts with your bank in New York. You are a gentleman of experience, Herr Whitford. You understand how these things must handle. Be handled, that is to say. Excuse my English if you please."

At the moment J. Aubrey did *not* please. He sniffed. Loudly.

"I can assure you, Herr Whitford, your funds will be most safe with us. I cite in example our conservative . . . um, uh . . . our conservative . . . with your deposits, I mean to say . . ." Kimmel floundered for the right word, said something in German, gave up with a shrug and lamely went on. "You see how cautious we be presenting ourselves, Herr Whitford. This is your assurance of care in our hands. We do for you no less than we do with every man, woman and child in this town, ja? Very safe. It is the . . . foundation? That is the word I wish? . . . the foundation of the Kimmel bank, the security, the safety of your money with us. We agree to accept your drafts in deposit. At once, Herr Whitford, you receive interest. Very good interest, Herr Whitford. Three percent per annum. We compound interest every month. Never have we failed to pay. You ask anyone. Very secure, we are. We send your drafts to New York the very soonest way, Herr Whitford. Coastal boat to New Orleans. Fast packet ship to New York, ja? I will enclose with this a note to my friend Herr Munk asking the speedy return. Then I mail to you drafts or coin by way of El Paso del Norte, ja? I have friends there also, Herr Whitford. Very fine gentleman name of Señor Jorge Guzman. A colleague, so to speak. Very wealthy. Fine gentleman. What they call a grandee. Him I trust. Him you trust. He will arrange everything between us, treat you very well, act as my agent for you. Is no problem, Herr Whitford. Six weeks, eight at the most, I can send the confirmation to you in El Paso del Norte." Kimmel spread his hands. He did not smile.

J. Aubrey frowned again. "The world has come to a pretty pass, sir, when a gentleman's word—nay, sir, his very signature on paper—will not suffice in a matter of business such as this."

"I agree, Herr Whitford, most certainly I agree, but my fadder and I have our depositors to think of. Ve can do no less for them than is required. I hope you understand. If not . . ." He shrugged. "You are free to do as you think best, Herr Whitford."

"I haven't cash in hand, sir, to pay the merchants here. Because, I might add, of the advice of your banking colleagues in New York City. It was at their recommendation that I chose to travel with drafts rather than specie. I now find, sir, that their advice was *most* unsound, at least insofar as this unpleasant little enterprise of yours is involved."

Kimmel's expression was unyielding. He didn't rise to the barb, and in fact may have missed registering it.

J. Aubrey stood. Hesitated a moment still, hoping even this late in the game that Kimmel would reconsider now that he was faced with the prospect of losing so large a deposit. The banker's expression changed not at all.

"Good day, Mr. Kimmel."

"Good day, Herr Whitford. If you have a change of the mind, I can be found at my home. I would accept your business after hours if you cannot delay."

J. Aubrey grunted and stalked away unhappily. Miserable damned penny-ante small-time backwoods banker, he grumbled silently to himself. His indignation was such that he very nearly believed that Kimmel had just turned down a deposit opportunity that would have paid benefit to the depositors in this hick community.

His humor on returning to the hotel was such that he very nearly forgot his engagement with Miss Grace Woolrich, and had to rush to bathe and prepare himself in time for supper.

FORTY

"SETBACK" is *not* synonymous with "defeat."

Oh, no. They are *such* different things.

J. Aubrey hummed softly to himself as he stood before the mirror in his hotel room. He fluffed the muttonchop whiskers that nearly hid his ears, inspected his eyebrows to see that no coarse hairs were straying into view, and made a face at himself to expose his teeth for close examination. White and even, but a gentleman could never be too careful in that regard. He dipped a forefinger into the water basin, then transferred it to a crystal cellar of salt that he'd had the foresight to carry upstairs after supper. He used the gummy wad of wet salt on his finger to vigorously scrub his teeth to their whitest and brightest. After all, a gentleman never knew . . .

J. Aubrey rinsed his mouth and spat into the chamber pot, then examined himself again. Quite perfect, thank you. And Miss Grace—she'd invited him to call her by the familiar term— would be meeting him directly. At *her* suggestion. He smiled. A walk on the square, she'd said. Listening to the oompah-pah band of the townsfolk, ho ho. Strolling in the moonlight was more like it, he suspected.

J. Aubrey felt *wonderful* now, thank you.

Why, he hadn't suffered a defeat here, despite that short-sighted ass Kimmel. Not in the slightest.

J. Aubrey had the name of Kimmel's favored colleague in El Paso del Norte, did he not? Is it not true that a name can be quite as favorable as an introduction?

That small-minded Kimmel hadn't thwarted him. Merely delayed him.

Señor Guzman—the name sounded vaguely German to J. Aubrey—should prove willing to accept the draft deposits and provide banking services—at least insofar as the señor would be permitted to believe—for the Whitford Expedition.

And, as no small bonus attached, there was the fact that Mr. Whitford and Miss Woolrich would be spending some weeks in close companionship en route to El Paso del Norte. Side by side on a swaying wagon seat, ha ha.

A man would have to be a fool to fail to appreciate an opportunity such as this.

J. Aubrey ran his cuff around the brim of his silk hat, checked his fingernails for cleanliness and tugged the tails of his coat smooth.

There was, he reflected, very little that was better than a moonlight stroll with a beauteous young woman to lend vigor to a gentleman's expectations.

FORTY-ONE

J. AUBREY felt his chest swell with prideful excitement and with—he was loath to admit it, yet it was undeniably true—with a genuine affection as well, when he returned to the Nimitz Hotel.

Miss Grace Woolrich. The name fairly sang in his thoughts. Miss Woolrich. Miss Grace. Dear Grace.

She was the most utterly remarkable, utterly charming young lady he'd *ever* met.

She was as she was named. Full of grace. Filled with beauty. Warm. Lively. Almost impish in her charm.

Her laughter was the sound of choral chimes in concert. Her smile was more dazzling than sunbeams.

Tonight they'd listened to distant music, but the music J. Aubrey heard came not from the bandstand, but from within his own wildly fluttering breast.

Tonight Miss Grace had stood close to him when they teased and whispered. Close enough that he could inhale the delicate fragrance of her scent. Close enough that he could perceive the warmth that emanated from her perfect form.

Close enough to reach out and . . . but, no. Not that.

For the first time in his entire adult existence, J. Aubrey Whitford had actually drawn back and declined to press that particular advantage.

Twice this evening her hand had inadvertently brushed against his. Once in a moment of laughter she'd touched his wrist. But innocently. He was sure of that. Miss Grace was a true innocent. It would have been churlish of him to take advantage of her.

With any other woman of his acquaintance . . .

But then Miss Grace was *not* just any other woman.

Miss Grace was . . . special. Perfect. Enchantingly fresh and delightful. She was not and would never be the low fodder for dalliance that he'd always *thought* he enjoyed. Miss Grace was far and away above all that.

He sighed and gave in to the delicious sensations of the moment, as his feet fairly floated above the soil. He mounted to the boards of the small porch at the front of the hotel, and his footsteps scarcely sounded there.

He felt . . . love? Could that be? It was a subject he had no experience with. Love was a word easily spoken, even more easily whispered. But felt? Never. Unless this inestimable joy was the very thing.

J. Aubrey quivered. He tingled. He wafted on air. He . . .

"Mr. Whitford?" The voice out of the shadows was soft and hesitant.

J. Aubrey snapped out of his self-imposed delirium, and focused his attention on the figure of a man who rose from one of the rockers that were scattered across the porch surface. The figure came erect and moved out into a spill of yellow lamplight that escaped from a nearby window.

"Ah, Daniel, I see it's you out here so late." The man was one of his expeditioners.

"I was waiting for you, Mr. Whitford," Daniel Warren said.

"Really?" J. Aubrey truly had no interest in this conversation. He would have much preferred to float up the staircase to his room and drift away into dreams of Miss Grace's eyes. Still, he was supposed to be the leader of these people. He would have to continue with the role, like it or not, until they reached El Paso del Norte. He stopped where he was and waited for Warren to join him.

"We heard about that banker, Mr. Whitford. Shame on the man is what we all say."

"That is very kind of you, Daniel. But however would you have heard of Kimmel's insulting behavior, sir?"

"Harry Field was talking to one of them Germans, Mr. Whitford. A storekeeper you bought a bunch of stuff off of."

That could cover a rather broad range of identification, J. Aubrey knew. Almost any merchant in town qualified under the description just given.

"He heard what you was wanting to do. Provision us out of your own pocket and everything."

J. Aubrey gave Warren a depreciatory smile and a small shake of his head, as if to say it was nothing. Which of course it was.

"Ever since that man back in Florida cheated you, Mr. Whitford, you been carrying us. Stuck by us and brought us all this way when a lesser man might of left us to fend for ourselves. Well, don't think we haven't taken notice, Mr. Whitford. Don't think we don't appreciate all you done for us. Every man of us knows. We've talked about little else since Harry told us what you tried to do and how you can't now because of that banker. Imagine, him not taking your draft. Why, it was good enough for that fellow in Florida. Just the word of a gentleman such as yourself should be more than good enough for any man." Warren shook his head sadly. "Well the loss is his, that's what we all say. That's the way those of us as knows you feel about it."

"It's kind of you to say so, Daniel." He wondered if soon, tomorrow perhaps, he might give a small speech of gratitude for the confidence his expeditioners placed in him. A few well-chosen words, say, while Miss Grace was in attendance? Surely it couldn't hurt J. Aubrey's cause were she to become aware of the regard the expeditioners held for him. "Thank you." He turned toward the front doorway.

"Oh, it wasn't just to tell you that that I waited up for you here, Mr. Whitford."

"No?" J. Aubrey stopped and turned back again.

"No, sir. I want you to know that we aren't just talking grateful, we're all willing to *do* grateful."

"I don't follow your meaning, Daniel."

"What I mean is, me and the rest of the fellows talked this over this evening. Already talked to Capt. Hay about it too. He'll be delaying our start in the morning long enough for the bunch of us to pass a hat around."

"Pardon me?"

"We're gonna pitch in and pay the bills with all them Germans, Mr. Whitford. Every single thing you ordered is gonna be delivered and paid for, and you're not to fret yourself a single minute about any of it. Won't a penny have to come outa your pocket for this."

J. Aubrey felt a moment of actual confusion.

Something very much on this order had been in J. Aubrey's mind all the way back in Florida, when he'd considered recouping his fortune by way of the cash the expeditioners carried with them. That plan was only abandoned when he came up with a better one to take many times that amount by way of the bank drafts.

Now . . .

He supposed he could go around the rooms tonight and take up the collection that was being so freely offered.

Volunteered to him.

Had there ever been a gamesman who wouldn't leap at an opportunity like this one? Why the marks were lining up and *asking* him to skin them.

None of them could actually know the total sum involved in J. Aubrey's purchases of convenience. He could claim any figure within three times of reason and likely collect it. Assess the expeditioners twenty, thirty, even forty dollars per man. Slide all that lovely coin into his pockets and be gone before the break of day.

This was what he'd been waiting for, wasn't it? If not in detail then certainly in substance.

This was his chance to take a healthy profit and move on to the next endeavor.

Except . . .

Except, of course, the amount that could be collected from the expeditioners would necessarily be far short of the face value of the bank drafts J. Aubrey had crafted back there in St. Augustine.

It would only be prudent for him to wait a little longer. Take his gain from Guzman rather than the expeditioners.

It would require only patience and a bit of travel for that to be accomplished. Wouldn't it?

J. Aubrey felt a burning in his cheeks and a lurch in his breast when he thought about leaving the expedition now.

Miss Grace was proceeding west to El Paso del Norte.

He could take a handsome profit in hand right here and now —if the truth be known, he could take a record sum this very night, rake in more tonight then he'd ever made on any single scam—but still and all . . .

Miss Grace was proceeding west to El Paso del Norte.

The prospect of not accompanying her on the long and possibly even dangerous journey . . .

J. Aubrey cleared his throat. It seemed oddly dry at the moment.

"I can't tell you how much this means to me, Daniel. In the morning I shall give you a list of the merchants I approached and the amounts due each of them. Would you be so kind as to complete the arrangements for delivery?"

"You don't want to do that yourself, Mr. Whitford?"

"I will trust the matter to your care, Mr. Warren." His throat was so dry now the words scarcely came through. Much better, he felt, that Daniel handle the collection and payment of the cash that would be involved. Some temptations, after all, are best not faced.

Warren beamed with pleasure at the thought of the confidence J. Aubrey placed with him. "Leave it to me, Mr. Whitford. I'll not let you down."

"I know you won't, Daniel," J. Aubrey said solemnly. He shook Warren's hand and, more than a little bemused by what he'd just done—what he'd just rejected—went inside the Nimitz and up to the room where his dreams tonight would have nothing to do with coin and currency.

FORTY-TWO

THERE WAS A FEELING, a certain sense, an undefined air or aura about the re-forming wagon train this morning that J. Aubrey felt but could not comprehend.

It was . . . livelier somehow. More friendly, perhaps. People smiled as they bustled. They waved. They "howdied" each other—an odd Texas custom that some of the expeditioners were adopting. Backs were slapped and hands shaken.

It was really quite unusual.

Or possibly—J. Aubrey considered it, wanted to reject it out of hand but couldn't quite—the difference was not so much among the members of the expedition and the accompanying wagon train, but with J. Aubrey's own perceptions of all these people.

It was true, he acknowledged silently, that for no good reason whatsoever he was this morning seeing his expeditioners less as sheep to be shorn, and more as people with whom he had traveled and travailed for a very very long way.

Always before, the individual members of the Whitford Expedition had seemed just so many pale orbs where faces might be inserted. So many mobile lumps of flesh with coin yet to be extracted from them.

This morning—the realization startled him and was mildly annoying—he was very much aware that it was old Pettijohn who sat on the bench just the other side of Miss Grace. That Bolliger and Hankins were on the seat behind, sharing a cheerfully whispered conversation. That Smith and his cohorts were dozing at the rear of the wagon. Why, he was even wondering how the odoriferous Mr. McArdle would be accepted among the passengers of the wagon further back. The dust that everyone would have to suffer through back there, behind the churning wheels of the lead rigs, might prompt the man to bathe. J. Aubrey found himself hoping so for everyone's sake.

All in all, he conceded, these expeditioners no longer seemed the faceless, formless mass they'd been to him when he packed them onto the old *Yucatán Princess*—so very far away that had been—with no intention whatsoever of ever seeing any of them again.

J. Aubrey sighed, and contemplated once again the marshmallow stupidity of the average human being. Imagine. Up and giving their money away for no good reason whatsoever. Taking up a collection and actually forking over good hard specie and perfectly valid currency, just like that.

And they'd gone and done it too. Last night's promises hadn't been shallow. This morning Warren had tapped on J. Aubrey's door practically at the peep of the dawning, asking for the promised list.

Now the wagon train was virtually surrounded by Fredericksburg merchants eager to deliver wares and accept payment. Out of Warren's hand. And in whatever quantity was required.

J. Aubrey was having no small amount of difficulty understanding this largess.

It was a stupid thing for them to do, dammit. He knew that. He knew he should feel contemptuous of them all, the silly sheep, for stepping in when they might have turned their backs and left the burden on him.

But dammit, he couldn't help feeling a certain amount of . . . gratitude? Um, no. He didn't think so. Gratitude was the sort of dumb, numb emotion felt by the sheep but never the shearer. If not that, then what?

He couldn't quite decide, and that puzzled him too.

J. Aubrey sighed again and concluded that were it not for the sterling presence of Miss Grace on the wagon seat beside him, he would have washed his hands of this whole affair and abandoned the lot of them. That was what they all deserved. Damned sheep.

"Isn't this exciting," Miss Grace exclaimed.

"Not half so exciting as your presence in our midst," J. Aubrey said gallantly.

"Hear, hear," Bolliger agreed from behind. "Well spoken, Mr. Whitford."

J. Aubrey smiled and nodded at the man. Bolliger reached up to scratch the side of his nose, and for the first time in all these weeks J. Aubrey noticed he was wearing a wedding band. Not that J. Aubrey'd ever heard him make mention of a wife. But then of course J. Aubrey never had bothered to engage in idle chitchat with any of the expeditioners. He found himself wondering now what would prompt a man to leave his home and family behind, and launch himself blindly toward the empty promises of a gold discovery a continent away. Was it hope that had brought Haywood Bolliger here? Or desperation? The man had had the wherewithal to gamble on the expedition, damn him. Surely he could afford to be taken by anyone smart enough to claim him for a prize. J. Aubrey turned back to Miss Grace.

"So many wagons," she breathed. "I had no idea."

J. Aubrey swiveled back toward the rear again and saw the wagon train as if for the first time. It was no wonder Miss Grace was so amazed. Once again the content of the train had changed dramatically since their arrival in Fredericksburg. But then this was virtually the last outpost of civilization, or so Squint Hay claimed. There would be little else of human habitation or commerce from here all the way to El Paso del Norte. And even less than that, Squint said, beyond there.

Most of the driven livestock had been destined for Fredericksburg. Now the loose stock consisted only of mules, a few horses and some long-legged, fully grown cattle. The goats were all absent, as were most of the cattle.

There were still Mexican *carretas* toward the rear, but every one of these now was drawn by either a horse or a mule. There were no slow-walking oxen permitted.

Each driving box on the large freight rigs now was occupied not only by the driver but by at least one helper as well. And J. Aubrey could see rifle and shotgun muzzles peeking out from their rests within the boxes also. The train now would be traveling as an armed convoy. That thought was rather disquieting. Not so much the fact of it but the necessity for it. Squint Hay was not the sort of man to arrange things without purpose.

The dark and vigorous little Texan was dashing his horse back and forth along the length of the assembled train, encouraging burghers and laborers alike to speed, as the last loading was completed.

Daniel Warren stood in the middle of it all, taking charge of the deliveries and disbursements with every bit as much vigor and devotion to his task as Squint showed toward his.

"Is that it, Dan'l?" Squint inquired from the back of the horse already lathered with sweat in the mid morning heat.

"I believe that's everything, Squint."

"Then climb aboard your rig, Dan'l. We're fixing to roll 'em outa here."

Warren hurried to the wheel of the lead wagon and clambered aboard, wedging himself in next to Hankins. He touched his hat toward Miss Grace and gave J. Aubrey a grin. Squint Hay wheeled his horse and made one last dash back to the end of the train. Then, apparently satisfied that all was finally in order, he rode briskly to the fore and yanked his sombrero off. He swept it grandly overhead, making a brave show for the townspeople who had come out to watch the leaving.

"Wagons-s-s-s-s, *ho-o-o-o-o-o!*"

FORTY-THREE

"YES, CAPT. HAY certainly does ride beautifully," J. Aubrey conceded with no pleasure whatsoever. Why, oh why, did Miss Grace have to admire so vulgarly physical an activity?

"Do you ride, Mr. Whitford?"

"I've not had the pleasure, Miss Grace."

"Pity," she said. "I know you would cut a splendid figure on horseback, Mr. Whitford."

He smiled. "And you, Miss Grace?"

"Oh my, yes. One could hardly grow up in Texas without learning to ride."

J. Aubrey found it immensely difficult to think of Miss Grace Woolrich as being a Texan. Texans seemed such an uncouth breed. Yet she was indubitably the proof of that pudding: there could indeed be exceptions.

He shifted a little on the bench and felt the warmth of her limb close to his thigh. The closensss was almost as unnerving as it was enjoyable. Even more enjoyable to him was the realization that the girl had to be aware of his nearness yet made no attempt to draw farther away.

J. Aubrey cleared his throat and wondered if he should speak to her now about walking out from the camp after supper, or wait and allow events to unfold as if by random chance. Better perhaps to not press her. Just let things happen. But make quite sure that things *did* happen. He smiled and leaned closer to hear —no hardship being nearer to her like that—when her lips parted to speak.

She was interrupted in whatever she was going to say by a shout far to the rear and a pounding of hoofs.

Miss Grace looked over her shoulder. Ahead of the train, Squint Hay heard the commotion also and wheeled his horse. J.

Aubrey looked around in time to see the column of wagons, carts and livestock being joined by a group of horsemen who were riding in pursuit at a hard gallop.

The horsemen made a ludicrous sight after seeing the likes of Squint Hay. These men were all plump and mustachioed, and they wore city hats and caps rather than the sombreros favored by Texans like Squint Hay. Yet the horsemen swept in on the wagon train with grim expressions and revolving pistols.

"Good Lord!" J. Aubrey interposed himself between Miss Grace and the armed riders as the men—he recognized them now, all of them Germans from Fredericksburg—galloped past the carts and freight wagons to the fore of the train.

The horses came to a sliding, dust-raising, head-tossing stop, square in the middle of the narrow road, immediately in front of the lead wagon where J. Aubrey and Miss Grace sat behind the driver.

"Hold up there," one of the Germans ordered.

J. Aubrey had a moment's difficulty recognizing the man, who was now wearing a linen duster and a derby hat, but the leader of this mad crowd was no other than their recent host Charles Nimitz.

"What is it, Charles? What's wrong here?" Squint requested as he came dashing back.

"This is a posse, captain," Nimitz announced loud enough for all to hear. "I've brought the town marshal and justice of the peace with me." He pointed toward two of the men who rode with him. J. Aubrey could see now that there were at least two dozen in the party. They seemed like fifty.

"Shouldn't you be getting after your man then, Charles?" Squint asked.

"We have already caught our man," Nimitz declared. "He is one of your people." The hotel-keeper turned and sent a dark look toward the men who crowded the passenger wagons.

"All that remains," Nimitz said, "is to prove which one of your men is the thief."

But there was no doubt whatsoever about Nimitz's meaning.

J. Aubrey blinked. Just barely in time he stopped himself from looking toward the rear of his own wagon where Smith and Black and Brown, the gentlemen of the surly dispositions and false names, sat all together.

He felt Miss Grace's slender hand creep cold and trembling into his, and absently he patted her wrist.

Whatever else happened, damn it, J. Aubrey intended to see to it that this delicate lady was not subjected to coarse sights or untoward language.

FORTY-FOUR

THE GERMANS dismounted and advanced menacingly toward the lead wagon, where J. Aubrey sat with Miss Grace close by his side. Squint Hay hurried to join them.

"Now what is all this about, Charles? I can't have you making wild accusations. What proof do you have that one of these men is a thief?"

"Silver," Nimitz declared. "From mein dining room it is gone. Silver I brought all the way from Germany. It is gone. Who else could take it, I ask you?"

Squint hurried to get in front of the mass of men from Fredericksburg, but there was a cold look in his eyes when he stared up at J. Aubrey and said, "This is a serious charge, Mr. Whitford. We may have to inspect the baggage of all your people."

J. Aubrey gulped and looked at the posse-men. At least the Germans were keeping their weapons in their belts for the time being. There was no brandishing of dangerous firearms, thank goodness. He patted Miss Grace's wrist again and this time could not stop himself from looking around at Smith, who was pretending to ignore the whole thing, although the big man certainly appeared rather red and flushed about his ears. Beside him Brown and Black were pointedly looking elsewhere too.

It occurred to J. Aubrey, and not for the first time, that Smith and his chums were running from some crime they'd committed back in New York. There was no telling what manner of loot might be uncovered in their luggage.

Still and all, dammit, Smith and his friends had contributed this morning with every bit as good a will as any other member of the Whitford Expedition. And they'd caused no harm or dissension during this long and difficult journey. Those three were entitled to every bit as much consideration as any other member of the group.

Besides, it would simply have gone against J. Aubrey's grain to roll over and peach on another player, no matter the game. Something like that simply was not done.

J. Aubrey cleared his throat and stood, facing Charles Nimitz and his burghers from the superior height of the wagon box.

"I am sorry, Mr. Nimitz. But I cannot believe that any of my expeditioners would have done so low a thing as you describe, sir. I shall not permit you to inspect the personal belongings of innocent men."

Nimitz said something in German, and the posse-men around him muttered.

"I am sorry, sir, but that is the way it must be. You may not conduct an inspection without the issuance of a proper warrant."

"You vant varrant, I giff varrant," a heavyset German in the crowd said. "I am chustice of peace, ja? I make varrant."

"And I vill serve it," said another man standing close to him. This one pulled a badge from his pocket and displayed it for all to see.

J. Aubrey frowned. He didn't want to leave his people unprotected. But he didn't want to put his own pinky into a crack either.

"No need for a warrant," Nimitz said now. "I see my silver, I think."

"What?"

"Ja, wrapped in mein own napkin. There."

Nimitz pointed.

His extended forefinger was aimed at a point directly beneath J. Aubrey Whitford's wagon seat.

And his expression was *very* cold.

"That is the man," another voice called out loud and firm.

The eyes were all aimed square and hard at J. Aubrey.

"Hang him," someone shouted.

"Bring za manacles."

"He must stand trial for vat he has done."

"Hang him."

J. Aubrey stood with his chin held high and willed himself not to look down at Miss Grace.

"Hang him."

The Germans crowded close around the wagon, and a dozen pairs of hands clutched and groped at him.

FORTY-FIVE

"HOLD IT!" Squint Hay barked. "Now you fellas just hold your horses here. You ain't gonna go an' hang nobody from my train without proof o' what he done." Squint pushed his way through the posse and placed his back to the side of the wagon, shielding J. Aubrey from the pawing, grasping hands of his accusers.

"Now everybody just calm down here. Back off and let the rest o' us see what's in that napkin." Squint looked up at J. Aubrey and asked, "Is that all right with you, Aubrey?"

"Certainly. I have nothing to fear for I have done nothing against these people." He was pleased and proud, and no small amount surprised, to hear that his voice did not crack when he spoke.

He hadn't done anything, of course. He knew that. But. . . .

"Back away now, just back away." Squint shooed the Germans back a few paces, and satisfied himself that they would keep the distance, before he motioned Charles Nimitz forward. Then the two of them together stepped up onto the wheel spokes, and Squint reached inside the rig to fumble on the floorboards under J. Aubrey's feet. J. Aubrey remained where he was, his back stiff and jaw firm, even though he could feel a palpitating tremor in his chest. If someone *else* had taken the silver and tried to hide it there . . .

"This's your napkin, all right," Squint conceded as he dragged a lumpy blue bundle into view. "Heavy too."

The napkin unmistakably was one of those that was used in the Nimitz Hotel dining room. It was a coarse linen cloth dyed a medium shade of blue. J. Aubrey recognized it. Surely so did everyone else who saw it.

Squint brought the napkin bundle out where all could see,

and held it awkwardly in both hands. It must have been heavy indeed. "Would you do the honors here, Charles?"

"I will." The hotel-keeper sent a look around at the scores of people—expeditioners and possemen and Mexicans alike—who were staring at this miserable tableau. Then he took hold of a corner of the napkin and folded it back.

There was a gasp of astonishment from Miss Grace.

And a groan escaped J. Aubrey's lips.

Nested within the fold of cloth was a packet of bright polished silver knives, spoons and forks. Several pounds of it at least.

The scrolled *N* initialing on the silver handles was more than enough to identify the silver as being the property of Charles Nimitz and his brand-new hotel.

"Hang him," that same voice called out again.

"No, try him first. Then we hang him."

J. Aubrey felt faint. He braced himself against the ordeal that was to come.

It was bad enough, damn it, to end on a note he hadn't earned.

It was all that much worse to think that Miss Grace Woolrich would be in attendance to see this inglorious ending to an illustrious career.

"Hang him."

Hands reached upward.

And this time Squint Hay made no effort to stop them.

FORTY-SIX

J. AUBREY felt himself being lifted bodily out of the wagon and brought down to earth.

He was aware, if dimly, that despite the anger in the words that had been spoken, the hands of these Germans were remarkably gentle in lowering him to his feet. The justice of the peace and town marshal flanked him, holding him by the elbows and half supporting him. He rather needed that support. There was a weakness in his knees and a certain hollowness in his belly.

"We will hold court here," a voice said. It might have been Charles Nimitz's. J. Aubrey did not know. And didn't particularly care either. He was in a state of mild shock, barely able to comprehend all that was happening to him now.

"How do you plead?" The question had to be repeated several times before it broke through the fog of J. Aubrey's thoughts to lodge in his conscious mind.

J. Aubrey drew himself firmly upright, lifted his fine leonine head erect, and said, "I have done you no harm. I plead innocence."

"Who will prosecute?"

"I will." That one J. Aubrey recognized. He was one of the merchants J. Aubrey'd done business with.

"What is your evidence?"

The prosecutor soundlessly pointed. Squint Hay frowned, but continued to hold the napkin full of silver in plain view of all.

"Guilty," the justice of the peace ruled in a loud, clear voice.

"Guilty," a chorus of German voices echoed.

The sons of bitches sounded *happy* about it, J. Aubrey marveled. He could hear giggling and laughter among those pronouncements.

They were going to hang him, and they were *happy* about it?

Why, that was enough to make a man angry. He stiffened, ready to throw a retort at them.

Before he could speak there was a sharp crack of noise from the back of the wagon and a voice almost as loud.

"Nobody's hanging nobody," the man who called himself John Smith swore.

Smith was standing on top of his wagon seat. He had a pepperbox pistol in his hand, and there was a thin stream of smoke issuing from one of the gun's just-fired muzzles. Black and Brown stood beside him, Black with a pepperbox in his hand too, and Brown holding a newfangled Colt's revolving pistol, much like the one Squint Hay carried openly on his belt. J. Aubrey had never noticed Smith or either of his friends having arms before this moment.

"Mr. Whitford, we ain't gonna let nobody railroad you like this. We seen you climb aboard this wagon a while ago. There wasn't nothing in your hands then. We don't believe you put that stuff under your seat." Smith waved the muzzles of his pepperbox in the general direction of the crowd of Germans. "We don't want to do anybody hurt, but we ain't gonna let you hang Mr. Whitford. Mr. Whitford, you slide outa here and grab you a horse. We'll make sure you got a lead on 'em before they can come at you again."

"Whoa, boys, this is gettin' serious," Squint injected. "Put those guns away before someone gets hurt."

"We'll put our guns away when Mr. Whitford is shut of here. Not a minute quicker. Ain't that right, boys?"

Brown and Black nodded their agreement. All three of the rowdies looked grim and fiercely determined to protect their leader.

"You don't understand, fellas," Hay insisted. "Charles, I think it's time to call off the joke here an' let everybody in on it."

"Yes, please," Nimitz said shakily.

"Put your guns away now, boys. Nobody's gonna be hurt. This here is . . . was supposed t' be . . . just a joke, see. Mr.

Nimitz had me plant that silver in th' wagon myself this morning. These boys from Fredericksburg was gonna hold a mock trial, see, an' have some fun an' then end up sentencing Aubrey t' a long and happy life an' load us down with sausages for tonight's supper. Those saddlebags over there are full o' sausages. It's a treat, like. Just funning, boys. Now let's don't let anybody get hurt over a makebelieve."

Smith frowned, then gave his chums a sheepish look and put his pepperbox back into the pocket where it had been concealed. Brown's and Black's guns disappeared just as quickly and just as completely.

J. Aubrey heard more than one long, relieved sigh from the Germans who stood close around him.

Apparently the burghers had been frightened every bit as badly as he before this game ended.

"We did not mean . . ."

"Never would we harm anyone or . . ."

"We only meant . . ."

J. Aubrey felt a chill roll up his spine. He shuddered, then regained control of himself and went back to the wagon to help Miss Grace down, while all around him there were people recovering from the startled shock of the false trial.

Within a few minutes there were fires going, and laughing voices surrounding the stalled wagon train. The Germans broke out their sausages for the Mexican women to grill for all, and flasks of brandy to wash the rich meat down.

The remainder of the day was spent in a party that too easily could have become a wake instead.

FORTY-SEVEN

J. AUBREY lay with his eyes wide open and a sharp-edged rock nudging his ribs. He was drunk enough that he didn't mind the rock all that much, but he really did wish he could get to sleep now. He was exhausted and still sober enough to realize it, yet could not stop the whirl and confusion of his thought processes.

The impromptu sausage grill and brandy bash had turned into a gala—crude and rustic but a gala nonetheless—that nearly rivaled the barbecue back in . . . whichever place that had been. Oh, yes. Victoria. It took him a moment to call the name to mind.

Camp tonight consisted of the side of the road where the spurious posse had caught up with the wagon train. Bed was no more than the nearest blanket laid down more or less where one stood. At the moment J. Aubrey was surrounded by the rasping drone of many snorts and snores, but he himself couldn't sleep.

He lay with his stinging, aching eyes aimed toward a field of clear and steady starlight, and just couldn't stop thinking.

Whoever would have thought it. Smith of all people. And Brown and Black too. Fugitives and perhaps felons as well. Certainly men with their own axes to grind, their own backsides to protect. Yet they'd declared themselves for him when they thought he would hang. For no *reason.* That was the part of it that J. Aubrey truly could not grasp. There was no profit in their participation, none save a considerable risk to themselves, had he in fact managed to escape and leave the three of them behind to face the wrath of the Fredericksburg posse without him.

Conduct like that was incomprehensible. Mad, even. Yet they'd done it. The three of them had gone and done it. And afterward they were celebrated and congratulated by all the other members of the expedition, many of whom claimed they would have done as much if only they'd been armed.

Mad. All of them.

J. Aubrey sat up in the chill air of the Texas night, and glanced aside toward the spot where Miss Grace Woolrich lay slumbering beneath a wagon.

For possibly the first time in his existence, J. Aubrey Whitford wished he could take his puzzlement to another in conversation.

He wished he could wake her. Talk to her. Ask her opinions. But of course he could not.

He sighed and listened to the snores. Heard the moist, whuffling flutter as a horse or mule snorted. Heard stamping of feet and soft groans in the stillness.

However does one thank a man for so bold and selfless a stand?

J. Aubrey honestly did not know.

He lay down again and closed his eyes. But he knew he wouldn't sleep.

FORTY-EIGHT

J. AUBREY stepped down from the wagon with a carefully contained groan. He was stiff and weary from travel and hard bedding, and he desperately needed a bath. But he could not complain. Not aloud. He turned with a smile and offered his hand to Miss Grace.

He was becoming frustrated in that quarter also. They had been side by side for several days now, but never alone. Always there were others within the sound of the slightest whisper. Drat.

"Thank you, Mr. Whitford."

"My pleasure, Miss Grace."

She alighted from the wagon with, um, grace. Her dignity was intact if not her garments. She too appeared quite as dusty and disheveled as J. Aubrey felt. The primary difference was that Miss Grace remained radiantly lovely. The rigors of travel rumpled but did not diminish her. J. Aubrey wished he could say as much about himself.

"We stop here for the night," Squint Hay announced from the back of his horse, even though it was barely the middle of the afternoon. They had halted hours earlier than usual. "Stay tomorra and tomorra night too. This creek is the last good grass an' water we can count on for a spell. Anybody wants t' set up tents that's fine, but keep 'em off the grass. That's needed for better'n a bed now. Stay over in them mesquites if you want your tents."

J. Aubrey heard a few mumbles of discontent from his fellow expeditioners. And no wonder. The ground beneath mesquite bushes, as they'd all come to learn too, too well, was littered with thorn and sharp sticks that were impossible to sleep upon with comfort. It was also true, though, that there was very little open space along the narrow creek where the stock could graze.

Texas, they were all learning, was not given to the green and grassy sward. Hardly.

For a time there, roughly from San Antonio to Fredericksburg, they'd all been deluded into thinking the land was not so bad as they first imagined, upon viewing the coastal plains and the thorny areas inland.

And actually it wasn't.

The truth was that it was considerably worse than those first impressions suggested.

The farther west they came, the drier and the thornier the land they traveled across.

A few years earlier the tales had been rampant about the Great American Desert and the hardships encountered by parties of gold-seekers racing to the California finds. J. Aubrey knew that nothing those reckless adventurers encountered could have been worse than Texas.

And now *he* was moving overland through desert? It was a sorry state he'd come to, through no fault of his own. He shuddered.

"Is something wrong, Mr. Whitford?"

"Not at all, Miss Grace," he lied pleasantly. "May I assist you with your accommodations?"

"How kind. Thank you." Her smile was almost enough to make the whole thing worthwhile.

One of the advantages of performing the labor of assisting Miss Grace with her camp each night was that J. Aubrey could lay out his own crude bed close to hers. For purposes of protection, of course.

He bowed and walked back to the baggage wagon to fetch their things. The women from the *carretas* were already busy laying out firestones and foodstuffs, while the children gathered wood and established the waist-high brush arbors that would become their homes for the next two nights. The drivers and the drovers were equally busy, rushing about under Squint Hay's orders to emplace the wagons in a circular pattern—a fort-like protection, Squint had explained, in the event of an Indian encounter—and to hobble or bell particular animals as required. That nightly requirement seemed quite natural now, but at first it had amazed J. Aubrey to learn that these people perceived individual mannerisms among the many mules and horses and cattle, and actually knew which ones were most likely to strike for freedom. Squint Hay, he was fairly sure, could actually tell one mule from another. Incredible.

J. Aubrey collected Miss Grace's canvas bedroll and small grip —she was traveling with little in the way of worldly possession, and he worried about her—and his own few blankets. He paused to pass a few pleasantries with Field and Pollack. The expeditioners invited him to join them later in a foray downstream to find a bathing spot in the creek bottom. Even McArdle had been prevailed upon to participate in the interests of good will and camaraderie. "Capt. Hay says there's a spot he knows of a quarter mile or so down where there's a hole deep enough."

"Delighted, gentlemen, if it proves at all possible," he assured them.

He even meant it. Aside from the improvements to both comfort and appearance that the bath itself would impart, these past few days he had been quite enjoying the company of his expeditioners. Even speaking with them. A situation like that was unlike anything he'd ever done before. Or wanted to. But then of course he'd been traveling in close confinement with this particular group of marks for an unusual amount of time. It was probably only natural that he should get to know these men better than he normally allowed. He never would have come to know these men either, if it hadn't been for that incident back in New York.

He smiled and excused himself, and made his way back through the beehive of camp-making activity slowly. Every few paces, it seemed, he had to stop again to visit or to chat.

The expeditioners, it seemed, had begun to bring the most insignificant of matters to him. And not their problems alone.

They brought up comments, observations, even their jokes to share with him. It was an experience he was finding oddly pleasurable. Along with the fact that of late some of them had begun referring to him as "Captain" Whitford. That had taken J. Aubrey somewhat aback, until Miss Grace pointed out that Squint was known as captain to the Mexicans by virtue of his leadership of the wagon train. Why then should Mr. Whitford not be afforded the same honorific in recognition of his expedition leadership?

Captain. It was a conceit J. Aubrey just might retain even after he milked the last he could from this venture and departed.

He frowned a little when he thought about that nearing moment. For some reason . . .

He shook his head angrily. A true gamesman *never* plays soft, damn it.

J. Aubrey felt ashamed of himself even for admitting the impulse.

"Thank you," Miss Grace said prettily.

"Do you have a spot in mind?"

"Over here, I think." She led him past a thick stand of prickly pear and pointed toward a small opening in the thorny brush.

"I'll put my things over here then," he said. "That way no one could approach you without passing my bed."

"You have been so . . . very kind to me, sir." Her eyes dropped away from his, and he thought he could detect a small blush on her cheek. J. Aubrey felt his chest swell.

He laid out her bed with care, kicking every last vestige of cactus far from the place where her slim form would rest, then hastily arranged his own blankets on the ground far enough away for propriety to be observed, yet close enough for him to hear should she call out.

"Could I presume upon your generosity further, Mr. Whitford?"

"It would be no presumption of yours, Miss Grace, but a privilege of mine, regardless of the request." He bowed elegantly before her. The turn of phrase was enough to draw another smile from her, as he had hoped.

She laughed lightly and said, "Mr. Hay tells me a group of the gentlemen will be going down the creek to bathe. He suggests if I want a bath I should walk upstream. But I wouldn't feel at all comfortable leaving the camp alone. Would it be possible for you . . . ?"

"I am honored by the confidence you place in me," he assured her. "It will be my pleasure to guard and protect you against all hazards." Again he bowed, and again she smiled. J. Aubrey felt his heart flutter and thump.

"I'll only be a moment. Let me get my soap and towel and . . . things."

J. Aubrey was quite sure that never in his life had he been happier than at this very moment.

FORTY-NINE

HE WAS TEMPTED. That was, he sadly acknowledged, the simple truth.

Never had he had to clamp so rude a control upon his baser impulses.

The rest of that truth, of course, was that never before could he recall ever *wanting* to control those impulses.

But now . . . Miss Grace was above any of that. She was better than that. She was . . . truly quite special.

J. Aubrey stood in the harsh sunlight with sweat trickling out of his side whiskers and down his neck, while mere feet away he could hear the cool sounds of splashing water as Miss Grace—he would *not* dwell on the too readily imagined scene, he simply would not—laved herself in a shade-dappled bend of the creek bottom.

J. Aubrey trembled. He quivered. He stood in rigid agony with his back turned away from the too-thin screen of mesquite withes, and tried with very limited success to refrain from thinking about the young lady who bathed nymphlike in the creek waters.

This was, he was sure, the absolute limit of human forbearance.

He managed. Somehow. Barely.

It was with an almost physical sense of relief that he finally heard her footsteps crunching dried leaves on the shore, and knew that she was toweling off, and would soon be decently attired once more.

He could control his eyes, but there was nothing he could do to block out the sounds. Or the visions they led to. He followed her every move and motion with keenly atuned hearing, until at last he heard the faint pat-pat-swoosh noises as she dusted off the skirt of her dress. He groaned softly then and expelled a long, slow breath. She was dressed again, thank goodness. He could relax now.

"Capt. Whitford? You can join me now if you wish."

He would sooner the invitation had come before she dressed than after. No, damn it, he wouldn't. Or maybe he would at that. He scowled—at himself, certainly not at Miss Grace—and turned to make his way carefully through the thin, whippy branches of the mesquites, so willowlike of appearance here where they were thoroughly watered, but so un-willowlike in the way they could snatch and wound the unwary.

"Do you feel better now?"

"Yes, thank you, much better." She moved a little closer to him and laid her fingertips on his cheek. He felt his heart lurch and tumble as it leaped into his throat. "I know I've deprived you of your bath with the other gentlemen. Would you care for me to move so you can . . . ?"

"Later. Perhaps." He wasn't sure he trusted himself with Miss Grace so near. Lord knew he certainly needed a bath, though. He'd needed one to begin with. And after the sweat he'd worked up while waiting those few steps distant from her, why, he undoubtedly smelled worse than one of Squint Hay's mules.

He took Miss Grace's hand. It felt tiny in his, cool and fragile. She was standing so very near. He felt a lump in his throat again, and wanted to get away from this place where he could not help visualizing the way she'd been just minutes ago. J. Aubrey cleared his throat awkwardly.

"Would you care to sit for a moment before we walk back? Just to talk, I mean. I, uh, noticed a small tree on that rise there. There would be shade and perhaps a breeze." He wanted to remain alone with her. But not on this particular spot.

"Yes, if you wish." Oh my, her smile was pretty. There was a hint of dimple on either side of her mouth. And her lips . . . He shivered.

J. Aubrey led the way, careful that she didn't snag her dress on the thorns, and climbed with her to the slight eminence that overlooked the bend in the creek bed.

There was a tree there as promised, and a flat ledge of pale, chalky rock. He brushed clean a place for her to sit and then joined her on the ledge. The ledge was not broad, but broad enough that he could have sat a little farther from her than he chose to.

Miss Grace's hand lay lightly on his wrist. Her face, so trusting, was lifted to his. Her lips were moist and her eyes bright. He felt himself being drawn to her almost as if beyond volition. He dipped his head slowly. She lifted hers. He could sense the delicate fragrance of her breath. J. Aubrey's heart rate sent the blood roaring through his ears.

A snapping twig and a harsh whisper of warning interrupted.

J. Aubrey snatched himself upright, his ears burning—to think that he'd been caught trying to impose himself on this lovely young lady.

Who was it who . . . he searched the sloping ground below their stone perch, trying to spot whoever it was approaching. He had to squint against the glare of the afternoon sunlight that covered the ground outside this shaded bower.

There, he saw. Coming up the creek seventy-five, perhaps a hundred yards away from the direction of the camp. He could see the figures only imperfectly at first through the brush, then clearer as they stepped around a wall of prickly pear and moved onto open ground. There were three of them. Smith and Brown and Black. Why, oh why, hadn't they gone down the other way with the rest of the expeditioners?

Smith stopped. Said something. Laughed. Received more laughter from his friends in return.

J. Aubrey frowned. Smith and his chums were laughing down there.

But from this distance J. Aubrey hadn't heard a speck of sound from their laughter.

How then had he been able to so clearly hear the crackle of their footsteps?

He felt Miss Grace shift position beside him. He glanced toward her in time to see her lips part to speak. He shushed her quickly with a squeeze of her hand and a warning shake of his head. She gave him a puzzled look, and he laid a finger against his lips.

Smith and Black and Brown were walking again, moving up the creek in what was obviously an idle stroll with no purpose in mind. But he could not hear them move. He saw them easily but heard nothing.

What then had caused those noises when he was about to kiss Miss Grace?

Miss Grace gasped and pointed, her other hand clutching at the base of her pretty throat.

J. Aubrey felt the blood drain from his head in sudden alarm.

There were Indians, wild Indians, hostile Indians, not twenty feet down the slope from where he and Miss Grace now sat.

FIFTY

J. AUBREY felt cold despite the heat of the day. Grace gasped again and pressed herself tight against him. He put an arm around her shoulders and held her close.

There were two Indians there. So close. He could see them plain now, crouched at the base of a small bush, and so silently immobile that they were easily overlooked. It was one of them, of course, he'd heard moments earlier.

J. Aubrey was sweating again. He tried to control his trembling. Even now he did not want Miss Grace to feel that and think him a coward.

The Indians were dark and deadly-looking. Nearly naked except for leather garments at their waists, garments that were almost like very long diapers suspended from a leather thong that encircled their bodies. Breechclouts, he supposed those were, but he had never actually seen one before.

Their lean bodies were sweaty—for some reason he hadn't thought that wild Indians would sweat the same as regular people do—and covered with dried filth. Neither of them had bathed in some time. Or was that coating of dirt deliberate. It was so heavy it almost looked like it might be.

Neither Indian was painted, he noticed. Weren't they supposed to paint themselves for war? Everyone said they painted themselves.

Oh, Lordy.

They had longish hair that was plaited and looked like it had been greased. Small, bright objects—shells perhaps or tiny carvings—were entangled in their hair.

One of them wore a leather vest.

Both had soft shoes on. Moccasins, those would be. The moccasins were plain and poorly fitted, not at all the gaudy objects J. Aubrey might have expected.

The terrible thing, though, was that these Indians were armed.

They carried bows in their hands, both of them.

The bows were little more than thick, stubby sticks of wood bent into a curve by way of a braided thong of some thin material. The weapons weren't at all like the gracefully curved and elegant things depicted in the woodcuts of popular magazines.

But then these bows were real.

And there were real arrows clutched in the left hand of each of those Indians.

Each had an arrow—just as crude and makeshift an object as their bows—fitted to their strings, ready to fire. Each carried more arrows in his fist. One held three arrows, the other four. For some reason J. Aubrey's attention was closely drawn on that particular point. Some reason? For rather good reason, actually. He could too keenly imagine what one of those splintery things would feel like if it were to penetrate his body.

It would be even worse were one of them to shoot Grace with an arrow. The thought of an ugly protrusion like that entering her delicate form . . . J. Aubrey shuddered.

Grace moved again, drawing back on the little ledge that had seemed so peaceful and loving a place just moments earlier.

J. Aubrey stopped her. The slightest movement could give them away. The faintest scraping of cloth over stone. The tiniest pebble dislodged. The crackle of a single leaf. Anything.

They were safe now only because the Indians' attention was focused on Smith and his friends, who were still strolling along the creek.

Brown said something, and the others laughed. Black picked up a stick and tossed it into the water. Smith punched him playfully on the shoulder, and Brown laughed about something. They were close enough now that J. Aubrey could hear faint sounds of their bantering play.

The Indians remained low behind the shelter of the brush with their arrows poised.

Why, those sons of bitches were waiting in ambush.

They intended to murder Smith and Brown and Black.

The enormity of that hadn't penetrated J. Aubrey's thoughts until this moment.

Those bastards were going to murder three innocent men.

J. Aubrey sat upright on his rock, scarcely aware now of Miss Grace clinging to his side.

The Indians were concentrating on the men they knew to be approaching. Neither of them had looked up the slope toward J. Aubrey and Grace.

J. Aubrey bit at his underlip and steeled himself. He lifted his free arm as high as he could and slowly waved it back and forth.

If he could attract the attention of one of the men down below he might be able to warm them. Point to the danger and motion them back. Something.

He waved, but none of the expeditioners was looking toward the top of the slope any more than the damned Indians were.

Smith and his friends meandered on, completely oblivious to the life-threatening danger that lay ahead.

They were closer now. Fifty yards or so.

How far could a bow and arrow shoot with accuracy? J. Aubrey had no idea.

If the men came on as they were, they would pass within fifteen or twenty yards of the hidden Indians.

Too close, that was sure. J. Aubrey doubted there was any hope that the Indians might miss at that distance.

Besides, if Smith and Brown and Black somehow escaped the ambush, the Indians would no longer be intent on watching the narrow area beside the creek. The Indians would be free to look around then. Surely then they wouldn't fail to see J. Aubrey and Miss Grace behind them.

Sweat rolled and stung on J. Aubrey's cheeks and neck.

He found himself wondering if he and Miss Grace would remain safe here if the Indians succeeded in their scheme and slaughtered those men down there. Would they rush down to scalp and rob their victims? Even if they did, would that diversion be enough to permit J. Aubrey to get Miss Grace safely away?

That was really the question, wasn't it.

He knew he would gladly sacrifice his own life in exchange for Miss Grace's safety. And John Smith's and Brown's and Black's too, if he had to.

But would that bloody offering even be enough to satisfy the savages?

He shuddered.

He could all too well imagine what would happen to this marvelous young woman at his side if those Indians discovered her.

He would *not* permit that to happen.

J. Aubrey sat there, uncertain, while every passing moment brought the three laughing expeditioners closer to disaster.

Smith and Black and Brown, of all people. The very men who had stood firm on his behalf when they thought he would hang. If he warned them, Miss Grace would die. If he did not . . .

He closed his eyes tight for a moment and tried to control the pounding in his breast.

He was frightened. Dear Lord, he was frightened. No, dammit, he was scared. Pure and simple, scared to the point that he was afraid he might foul himself. He'd never been a brave man. Never wanted to be one either. But now . . .

Smith pointed to something upstream, toward some plant or object that lay beyond the lurking Indians in their ambush.

"I'll race you to it," Brown said. His voice came clear up the slope to J. Aubrey's agonized ears.

"On three," Smith said, "and we'll all go."

The three of them stood there for a moment, each man trying to jockey for an advantageous position ahead of the others, and each man determined that no other should be allowed in the fore.

"One," Smith said.

The Indians glanced at each other, and one of them nodded. "Two."

The Indians raised up in their crouch and drew their bow-strings back toward their ears.

"Three!"

FIFTY-ONE

THE THREE EXPEDITIONERS yelped happily in their igno-
rance of the danger. On the shout of "three" they sprinted forward up the creek bank.

Above them the dark and deadly Indians came to their feet
with bows drawn and arrows aimed.

Above the Indians, J. Aubrey could no longer contain himself.

With an ear-splitting roar that startled even himself, he
bounded in huge leaps down the rocky slope.

"Run, Grace, run!"

He covered the distance to the Indians almost instantly with
that shrieking charge, and threw himself bodily onto them.

Both Indians had turned but were immobilized—startled,
frightened, it did not matter the cause—at the apparition of a
white man in top hat and cutaway coat descending on them in a
mad attack.

Neither Indian had time to reverse his bow and aim a shot at
J. Aubrey before he was onto them.

He threw himself sideways in an effort to strike both at once,
flinging his body atop them, and swept the two Indians off their
feet.

The three shapes tangled and fell together down the hillside.

J. Aubrey heard a guttural "whoosh" as the breath was driven
from at least one of the Indians. There was a crash and crackle of
splintering wood, as a bow or arrow shaft was caught beneath
one of the falling bodies and gave way.

He fell on top of one, the Indian's body cushioning J. Aubrey's fall onto the unyielding earth. He'd lost track of the
other.

Something banged into the side of his head, and there was a
sharp pain in his side. He'd been stabbed, he guessed. He struck

out furiously with fists and elbows and knees. As long as there remained life within him he would continue to protect the girl who was his responsibility here.

"Run, Grace!"

He hadn't time to consciously register vision. The world about him was a whirling blur of color and motion.

He pummeled whatever he could reach, cursed once when his flailing hand hit rock, smelled rancid grease rubbing against his nose and bit down mightily on whatever portion of whatever Indian it was within reach of his teeth. He was rewarded with a howl of pain and a blow to the side of his head that brought a ringing to his ears.

"Run, Grace."

Something smashed into the side of his leg. He rolled, punched, kicked at something near his feet.

"Ouch, dammit."

J. Aubrey's eyes were squeezed tightly closed. He couldn't bear to see his own blood. The body he was lying on writhed and tried to wriggle away. J. Aubrey grabbed hold with hands and teeth and sought to do all the damage he could.

He thrashed and battered and cursed. Snarled and spat and did his best to smash a human form into pulp.

He felt something pulling at his shoulders and rolled to meet this new assault, his arms wildly flailing and his breath heaving through his clenched teeth in great, raw sobs now.

Whichever one it was jumped backward, and he turned back once again to attack the one he'd been lying on.

"Jeez, cap'n, you can quit now, I think."

He blinked. Opened his eyes.

"What?"

Smith was standing warily nearby, peering down at him intently.

"What?" J. Aubrey repeated.

"I said I think you can quit now, cap'n. That Injun ain't moved lately."

J. Aubrey shivered and rolled off the Indian's inert form so he could sit upright.

The other Indian lay stretched out on the rocks a few feet away. He was bleeding from a gash in the side of his head. The bright blood mingled with the grease in his hair, turning the side of his head into a wet scarlet and purple mass. Brown stood over him. Black was busy collecting fallen weapons, the one unbroken bow and remaining arrows, and a pair of crude knives as well.

The Indian J. Aubrey had been so intent on pummeling was unconscious, his breath rasping and ragged.

J. Aubrey shook himself like a dog coming in from the rain.

He felt disoriented and unsure of where the haze of fury left off or reality began. It took him a moment and several deep breaths to be sure that the fog of his anger had cleared.

"I think one of them stabbed me." He looked down at his side. There was pain there but no blood. He must have fallen onto something by accident.

"You all right, cap'n?"

"I . . . think so, John. Thank you."

Smith took his hand and dragged him upright.

Miss Grace stood in an awed silence not ten feet away.

"I thought I told you to run," J. Aubrey complained.

Mutely she nodded. Her eyes were very wide and very bright. Her lips were slightly parted.

"That took nerve, Mr. Whitford. Bravest thing I ever saw any man do," Smith said. "They were laying for us, weren't they?"

J. Aubrey really didn't feel like talking about it at the moment.

He looked down at the two unconscious Indians and felt like throwing up. The only thing that kept him from it was the knowledge that if he did, Miss Grace would see and know him for the coward he actually was.

"They were, Mr. Smith," Grace said. "They had their arrows drawn, and Capt. Whitford attacked them barehanded. He saved you. He saved all of us."

"Jesus," Black said.

"Capt. Whitford is the bravest man there ever has been," Grace Woolrich declared. "I would take an oath to that effect, gentlemen."

"So would I, Miss Woolrich. So would we all."

"You think we should shoot these Injuns?" Brown asked. He had his gun out and looked like he was prepared to accomplish the deed if that was what Smith—or Capt. Whitford—thought best.

"I . . . don't think so," J. Aubrey said. He abhorred violence and had had quite enough of it for one day, thank you. Besides, there was the lady's sensibilities to be considered. And who knew, the sounds of gunfire might attract more Indians to take the place of these. "I think we should leave them where they are and get back to the train at once. We have to warn Capt. Hay that there are hostiles in the vicinity."

"Whatever you say, cap'n."

J. Aubrey walked shakily up the slope and gave Miss Grace his elbow.

He was still puffing and winded. But the truth was that he felt quite proud of himself now. And he was very much aware that there was something, something indefinable but quite bright and lively, in her eyes now when she looked at him. He squared his shoulders and tugged at the hem of his vest, and escorted her back to camp with all the dignity he could muster.

FIFTY-TWO

IT WAS LATE before J. Aubrey was able to retire that night, but he didn't mind. He had been the toast of the camp the whole evening long.

And Miss Grace had scarcely strayed from his side the entire time.

J. Aubrey had no idea what might have happened to the Indians. Squint Hay had led a party of armed men out to the site with Smith and company for guides—J. Aubrey certainly hadn't wanted to go and would not have permitted Miss Grace to go along even if she'd wanted to—but they reported there were no bodies remaining by the time they arrived. Either the Indians had recovered from their daze and dragged themselves away, or others of the tribe found them and carried them off for savage burial rites. Squint said they did that sort of thing. In spite of everything, murderous intent and all, J. Aubrey found himself hoping the former possibility was the case, but he likely would never know. He chose to believe that the Indians recovered their senses and walked away.

From this vantage point of time and distance, the whole thing seemed unreal to him anyway.

He stood, yawning hugely and aching in every muscle after the unaccustomed activity of physical combat, and made his excuses. Miss Grace, he noted, rose to leave the fireside at the same moment he did.

"Don't you fret yourself, Aubrey," Squint offered. "You'll feel tip-top come the mornin'."

"And so I shall to be sure, thank you."

Squint grinned and winked at him. J. Aubrey hoped—and chose to assume—the gesture had nothing to do with Miss

Grace's decision to retire at this time. Otherwise he should be forced to thrash Capt. Hay in addition to those two savages.

John Smith and his cronies got up as well. Smith's attentions tonight had been positively embarrassing, but all he said now was, "If there's an Injun alarm in the night we'll call on you first thing, cap'n."

"Consideration need only be taken so far, John. I would be content to leave the next batch to you." The remark brought a round of laughter from the men of the train, and J. Aubrey led Miss Grace through the crowded encampment.

The shape of the camp had changed quite a bit since it was discovered that the members of the wagon train were not the only inhabitants of this rough prairie at the moment.

The carts and wagons had been drawn into a more carefully defined defensive circle, and half the space contained therein was roped off for the benefit of the livestock. Ground that should have been covered with tents and bedding was now devoted to this makeshift corral. The human members of the train had to make do with what area was left.

At least Hay and the men had been considerate enough to allow Miss Grace sole possession of her prickly pear enclave. And as few beds as possible had been laid close to J. Aubrey's. He thought that considerate of them. There would be people close enough to the screening prickly pears for conversation to be heard, but at least Miss Grace would not be on public view as she slept.

"Are you feeling better now, Aubrey?" In the firelight he thought he saw her blush a little. But she did not amend the informality of addressing him by first name alone.

"Much, thanks." He was still abraded and sore, but he did indeed feel better now than he had. "I fear my costume suffered far more than my person."

He made a rueful face and reached up to touch the crown of his silk hat. The hat was his pride and joy, but he had to conclude that it would never be the same. Some one or some thing this afternoon had battered it flat. It showed creases and wrinkles the hatter never intended and fashion never allowed. Unfortunately it was probably the only such article to be found this side of New Orleans. And New Orleans was a world away from a country where wild Indians might attack with neither warning nor provocation.

Miss Grace laughed and linked her arm into his, walking now so close at his side that he could feel her hip bump lightly against his. "It isn't your costume that matters, you know. It is the quality of the man within that counts."

This time it was J. Aubrey's turn to blush. He was sure that he was. He could feel the heat of it illuminating his ear-lobes and radiating outward.

"Your tail is ripped a little," Miss Grace said.

"Pardon me?"

She laughed. "The tail of your coat, silly. It's rent just the least bit. I have a sewing kit in my valise. Would you allow me to make the repair for you? I'm not a very good seamstress, I'm afraid, but it would please me to be able to offer that small service."

"I am honored that you would even consider it."

"In that event, sir, the honor may be of greater value than the service. You haven't seen my stitches yet. But I shall certainly do my very best."

They reached the opening to the miniature clearing where her bed lay, guided there by the light of lowering fires in the wagon compound.

J. Aubrey stopped at the entrance, which was no more than a narrow break in the prickly foliage.

He wanted to kiss her. He knew he shouldn't, even though they had been so close to it earlier.

He hesitated a moment too long, and Miss Grace slipped lightly away to the interior of the clearing. She moved so daintily that he could hardly hear her passage even on this rough ground.

"Good night, Miss Grace."

"Aubrey." Her voice came to him in a soft whisper out of the darkness. And again she had chosen, deliberately this time, to use his given name only.

"Bring me your coat, Aubrey. I couldn't possibly repair it if you'll not let me have it."

"It's too dark for sewing now."

She laughed. "I keep telling you, you haven't seen my stitches. Night might improve them. Besides, if I have it already to hand, why, I shall be able to set about my task immediately I awaken."

J. Aubrey trembled. This invitation had nothing to do with coats and sewing. Of that he was sure.

Yet even now he hesitated.

This wasn't *like* him. Under any other circumstance he'd ever encountered he would by now be halfway unbuttoned. Yet he stood at the mouth of the clearing like a fool.

Miss Grace did not speak again. He knew she would not. She was a girl of great pride.

With a poorly contained groan that was more disappointment with himself than anything else, he stepped inside the bucolic boudoir of rock and cactus.

"The coat if you please," Miss Grace whispered.

He removed it. Felt her small hand take it from him and lay it aside. Then she was standing before him again, so close they nearly touched.

He took her into his arms, and he was trembling like a boy stealing a very first kiss, when he gently placed his lips against hers.

Grace felt small and warm and delicate inside the circle of his arms.

He discovered that she was trembling too.

"Oh, Aubrey, I . . . I'm so sorry."

"Sorry, my dear?"

He felt more than saw her hesitant nod. It seemed terribly dark here after the firelight.

"I'm not at all the kind of girl you think I am, dear Aubrey. I only wish I were. For you."

J. Aubrey felt a jarring chill. "No!" he pleaded. "Don't wish that. Never wish for a thing like that. Do you believe for one moment that I could, that I would dishonor you? even if you demanded it of me? No, dear heart. I'd have you no way but who and what you are. Believe me about that, dear. I'd not have you brought low for . . . for anything."

She clung to him. He could feel the heat of tears where she laid her pretty face against his chest.

"I wish I could be the girl you think I am, Aubrey."

"No, dear, but . . . I wish I were the man you believe me to be."

"Oh, aren't we the fine pair," Miss Grace moaned.

"Are we not," J. Aubrey agreed.

"You will hate me in the morning," she said.

"Never," he swore.

"Yes. I know you will."

"I'll not, my dearest. Because nothing will come of our meeting tonight. Nothing but purity and innocence. I swear it to you. I'll take no advantage of any girl so fine and dear as you are, my darling Grace."

She said nothing, but he could feel the sobs wracking her tender breast.

She was tearing herself apart. And for him. For a man who wasn't truly fit to wipe the mud from her shoes.

She would offer her all to him. That great and priceless gift was all the treasure the girl possessed. Worse than casting pearls to the swine, that would be. No man who was not an utter cad would do such a thing to her.

J. Aubrey felt a tear of his own gather heat behind his eyelids.

Only a cad? Then who better than J. Aubrey Whitford to prove his own despicable nature.

Not . . . this . . . time.

He placed his fingertips beneath the point of her pretty chin and lifted it. Looked deep into her eyes with starlight winking and reflecting there. Touched his lips only briefly to hers once more.

Then—*this* was the bravest thing he'd ever done; those Indians were not so much as in the running for that honor—turned and walked alone to his rocky bed.

FIFTY-THREE

J. AUBREY woke with a groan that turned into a yip of pain as all of yesterday's bruises and abrasions pierced him with the very first movement of his stiff and aching frame.

He felt like gremlins and leprechauns had spent the entire night beating him with sticks. Big ones.

He rolled over onto his face and tried burying his eyes in the crook of his arm to keep the newly rising sun out of his eyes, but that did no good. He was wide awake now, and the pains in every joint and muscle would surely keep him that way.

Better to endure the suffering with a full stomach and hot coffee, he decided, than lie here and take it straight.

Best yet, maybe Squint would have a tot of that German brandy left over from the sausage gala. A few swallows from one of those flasks would make the world a better place indeed.

Grunting and groaning, J. Aubrey came to his knees and wedged open first one eye and then the other. They felt glued shut and gave up the fight only with difficulty.

"No!"

The exclamation escaped his lips quite unconsciously, as he abandoned his concerns for the nagging pains and sprang to his feet.

He'd slept in trousers and smallclothes, and now he took a step forward without thinking, then quickly did think, and retreated to the relative safety of his blanket. He balanced on one foot and then the other as he hastily brushed away the thorns that were invading his soles, then jammed his feet into his shoes without bothering with stockings or spats.

"No," he whispered softly to himself in an anguished but futile complaint.

From where his bed was placed he could look directly into Miss Grace's prickly pear boudoir.

It was empty.

There wasn't a sign of girl or bedroll or valise to be found there.

Only J. Aubrey's own maroon cutaway lying carefully folded on the ground where yesterday he'd placed the lady's bedroll.

The coat.

And a paper pinned to its lapel.

Almost in tears, J. Aubrey dashed forward to grab up the cutaway and the note that it carried.

FIFTY-FOUR

"MY DEAREST AUBREY:

"I know you cannot forgive me. You mustn't try. Accept simply that I am unworthy of you. You see, I truly was not the sort of girl you believed. I would have tried to play that role, but it would have been a sham and I could not do that to you. I can no more change than the flowers not blossom in spring or the rivers turn back against themselves.

"I tried at the very least last night to give you some small repayment for your loss but you, dear Aubrey, are too fine and generous a soul for that.

"The true loss is all mine, dearest heart. The truest gain all yours.

"Please do not try to find me. My name is not Grace. I only wish for both our sakes that it were."

The note was not signed.

But then it needn't be.

J. Aubrey bent his head to trembling hands so he could weep.

At least, he tried to bend his head to trembling hands. His hands were, at the moment, occupied with holding the maroon cutaway.

Old habit made him pull the coat on, rather than drop it onto the thorny soil of this Texas hell where morning birds sang, not knowing that their sounds should have been silenced on this awful day.

J. Aubrey thought about weeping now that he was free to do so.

But there was something that did not feel quite . . . right.

It took him a moment to puzzle it out.

And then he realized.

He reached inside the coat to the inside pocket. There! That was what was bothering him.

The pocket was empty. The lump of paper he'd carried there for so long was gone.

Thousands of dollars in bank drafts—spurious, to be sure, but no one else knew that—were missing.

J. Aubrey scowled. Opened the note and read it a second time.

Forgive. Unworthy. Not the sort of girl. Repayment for loss. The true loss.

Why . . . *dear Miss Grace stole his bank drafts and escaped in the night.*

J. Aubrey looked up toward the sky. Back down to the note. Up again. Re-read the message.

He felt his chest swell.

The whole morning turned brighter.

He threw his head back and began to laugh.

FIFTY-FIVE

J. AUBREY sat perched atop the horse and peered down toward the ground. It was an *awfully* long way down there, wasn't it. He shuddered to think what would happen if a person were to fall. And such a precarious seat a saddle was. He'd had no idea.

There would be no changing his mind, though. If balancing on the back of a dangerous beast like a horse was what was required, well, that was what it would have to be.

Besides, he had other things to think about right now. Important things. His mind had been a furious whirl practically from the first moment he'd realized what Grace had done and what her note conveyed.

"You're sure I can't pay you for this?" J. Aubrey asked.

"Naw, horses is cheap in Texas, Aubrey. You use 'im how you please an' welcome to 'im," Squint said. "Just mind you treat that girl right, hear?"

"I shall," J. Aubrey promised solemnly.

Not that anyone else in the train knew what had really happened last night. He was sure they all believed he had been cad enough to take advantage of the girl and now was seeking to set things right.

Well, he supposed they weren't entirely wrong at that. Let them think it. He certainly wasn't going to mention to them anything about missing bank drafts.

A thing like that, why, rumors could spread. Someone might question those drafts when he and Grace—or whatever she chose to be called by then; it wasn't like his name was really J. Aubrey Whitford either—tried to cash them.

He was quivering with anticipation now. He'd never ever

before felt so completely alive, so totally filled with optimism and enthusiasm and . . . and *every*thing.

This was the most wonderful thing that could ever happen to him.

And the best part of it was that he recognized and appreciated the fact even as it occurred.

Grace could no more change than the flowers could decline to bud, she'd said. J. Aubrey could not change his nature either. He'd had his moments of weakness in the recent past. But they'd been moments only.

Oh, in the future he might see his marks in a different light. A softer and gentler light. He might appreciate them more, and skim from them gently.

But now . . .

Now just as quickly as he could find that wonderful girl who'd called herself Grace, J. Aubrey Whitford would no longer be alone in the life that was his.

The possibilities were without limit.

He could teach Grace everything he knew.

Not callow theft but elegant gamesmanship.

They could work as a team.

They could . . .

"Aubrey."

"Yes, John?" Smith stood beside the stirrup looking up at him, with his cronies Brown and Black close at his side as always.

"You sure you won't reconsider an' take this?" Smith withdrew the ugly little pepperbox pistol from his pocket and extended it.

J. Aubrey chuckled and shook his head. "For the last time, John, I won't accept it. Although I thank you for the offer. I wouldn't know what to do with a thing like that anyway."

Smith frowned. "Poor repayment for all you done if all we can send you off with now is one o' Squint's horses an' a saddle."

"Repayment? None is needed, John. Not from you nor from

any other man of our expedition. I'm the one to be grateful to all of you for understanding and allowing me to leave you here so far from the Baja."

For one brief moment J. Aubrey was very nearly tempted to tell them that there was no Baja gold discovery.

Fortunately, he came to his senses in time and kept his mouth closed on that subject.

That would only tap a keg that was better left untouched.

Besides, who was to say that these very gentlemen might not make the gold strike that could be hidden there within that foreign soil.

Let them go on. Great things might come of their adventure yet, wherever they ended up, without his expertise to guide them.

He laughed and shook their hands, as one by one the members of his ill-fated Baja expedition filed past to say goodbye to their leader.

"You take care o' yourself, Aubrey."

"You too, Squint. Take care of my people. They are good men, one and all."

"I'll taken 'em all the way t' the damn Baja if'n they don't mind waitin' whilst I visit my sister a spell," Squint pledged. "Just mind you take care o' that pretty lady."

"Oh, I shall. My word on it," J. Aubrey said with genuine sincerity.

He picked up the reins awkwardly in two hands, took a moment to examine them and then shrugged.

After all, how difficult could it be to learn to ride a stupid beast. Or to find one pretty girl in the West.

J. Aubrey Whitford had no doubt whatsoever that he could manage both tasks.

"Get along, horse. Move." He bounced up and down on the saddle seat as he thumped the horse in the ribs with the heels of his shoes. "Get along now."

The horse turned its head to give him a look that he interpreted as one of annoyance, then snorted and shuffled down the road at a trot.

J. Aubrey clung to the saddle horn with both hands.

He would have waved goodbye to the gentlemen of his Baja expedition except that he didn't think he could maintain his balance if he once let go.

AUTHOR'S NOTE

DESPITE THE WAY things seem, I am not quite the liar you may believe. There really was a Nimitz Hotel in Fredericksburg, Texas, in 1852. It was operated by Charles Henry Nimitz, grandfather of the World War II American naval genius Admiral Chester Nimitz. Moreover, Charles Nimitz was a practical joker. One of his favorites was indeed to hide hotel silver in his guests' luggage for the purpose of pulling a prank much as the one that so nearly went awry here.

Apart from that tiny bit of historical accuracy, however, I must alas confess to being the liar you undoubtedly thought, for the remainder of the story is no more true than J. Aubrey Whitford's scams. But all of them could have been, eh?